Explicit Erotic Sex Stories

Our Home (Lesbian)

A possibility experience and two hearts finding their direction home

Pamela Vance

This is a work of fiction. Names, character, places and incidents are either the product of the author's imagination or are used fictitiously, and any resemblance to actual persons, living or dead, business establishments, events or locales is entirely coincidental.

@ COPYRIGHT

*****

Chapter one: Wrong spot, wrong time.

I love running, the beating of my feet on the asphalt beneath, and the way that pushing my body past the purpose of fatigue clears my head and encourages me think straight. The manner in which I can generally feel the perspiration leak from my each pour, yet I couldn't care less. Running is my upbeat spot, the one thing in the entire world I know can't be detracted from me.

Today was the same, my feet were beating the walkway underneath them as I ran at a consistent speed through the school grounds. The fall air around me is cool and fresh and I inhale it in by the lung full. I've been here at NYU for half a month, beginning my first year where I'll be studying music hypothesis. My folks aren't excited with my field of decision, yet I worked my rear end off all through secondary school to get a full scholastic grant to a school this great, so I ought to at any rate have the option to consider something I'm enthusiastic about.

Music impacts through the earbuds I'm wearing muffling a great deal of the clamor around me meaning I can well and really lose myself to my #1 breathe easy. I'm so invested in my own contemplations and the mood of my legs that I don't see the blondie transforming the corner towards me and I run into her at max throttle, viably thumping her straight on her rear end.

We fall wrecked of arms and legs, the espresso she's holding spills from the container covering us both in the lukewarm, earthy colored fluid. Some way or another in the conflict I wind up floating over her gazing down into the most flawless green eyes I think I've ever had the joy of seeing, she flickers at me and briefly I neglect myself "shit..." I mumble.

"You could state that again..." she says in what is unmistakably a British pronunciation. I turn ruby when I understand our position and propel myself up and off her, holding out my hand to help her to her feet.

I hazard a second to take in her appearance and the young lady is shocking, marginally taller than me, however constructed thin. Sandy light hair pulled once more into a free bun, ringlets of her reasonable hair outlines her face, separated blushing lips that seem as though they were made to kiss. I flicker a couple of times and swallow seeing how dry my throat and mouth has become "I'm so grieved about that. I didn't see you coming..."

I watch as she feigns exacerbation at me and peers down at her destroyed shirt "incredible, well now since you weren't watching

4

where you were going. In addition to the fact that i will be late, my shirts demolished. You know what..." I raise an eyebrow at her and cockerel my head aside. What the heck is this current young lady's concern? I get I wrecked her, yet I was sorry... "disregard it. Screwing yanks..." and with that she's gone leaving me watching her egotistical ass leave.

"All things considered, screw you as well!" The young lady's dazzling, yet she's sort of an ass as well. I don't need to time to harp on my spat with the chick with the incredible ass however crap disposition. I need to make a beeline for my quarters to prepare for class, since this evening, I start work at the bistro nearby.

At the point when I return to my room my flat mate Clara is sat crossed legged on her bed with her nose covered in a book. The sight makes me smile somewhat, my freshly discovered companion is amazingly diligent, more so than me yet she is all that one could need in somebody with whom you share a space. She's clean, tranquil and chivalrous. In any case, don't allow appearances to trick you, since she likewise has a devilish awareness of what's actually funny which I revere. "Great run?" She asks without turning upward from her book, I grin at the highest point of her head and kick my running shoes off.

"Definitely it was incredible, until I ran into this self important little bitch with an extraordinary ass however a crappy mentality. That is to say, I said I was heartbroken? In any case, she goes off on this tirade and heads out in different directions with a 'screwing yanks' remark." Clara raises her eyes to meet mine and she characteristics an eyebrow.

"My gracious my, she absolutely has scoured you some unacceptable way..." she cocks her head aside and studies me such that makes me become flushed a bit "or possibly that is something you'd be open as well?" I feign exacerbation and throw the shirt I had quite recently taken off at her prior to shedding my running jeans and wrapping my clothing clad body in a towel.

"Try not to be such a perv, I'm going for a shower and afterward I will class." Picking up my shower caddy I pivot suddenly and head for the entryway.

Fortunately the remainder of the day goes on without another altercation with the young lady I pushed over earlier today. Notwithstanding, I'm struggling shaking her from my contemplations. I've realized I was gay for quite a while, and experiencing childhood in Texas has been... hard no doubt. Houston isn't the most tolerating place on the planet so whenever I was allowed the chance to concentrate here I took it with two hands and ran. I've had sweethearts, hurls however nobody has had the very impact that she appears to have.

My psyche continues to flitter back to the manner in which the sun hit her eyes making them sparkle like emeralds, her hair shone like spun gold and she resembled a late spring morning. Her lips, gracious sweet Jesus her lips. I figure I could spend a lifetime adoring those ideal lips. The piece of me that kept on having these steady contemplations, musings that filled my cerebrum with her and diverted me from my examinations throughout the day, didn't mind that she was an ass. That part continued telling the objective piece of my mind to quiet the fuck down and let it have a great time.

When I was going to begin work I had figured out how to talk myself around to pushing her out of my considerations and to focus on bringing in some cash. Venturing into the bistro I was right away hit with the smell of new ground espresso and the buzz of understudies talking among themselves. I weave my way through the packed floor towards the counter where I attempt to stand out enough to be noticed of the barista "pardon me?" Nothing, he's more keen on playing with the brunette toward the finish of the counter. I give him a second prior to rehashing myself somewhat stronger "pardon me?" This time he goes to confront me with a disturbed articulation.

"How would i be able to help ya?" I battle the inclination to feign exacerbation and grin as pleasantly as I can oversee at the over-built person who's unmistakably disrobing me with his eyes.

"I'm Kaitlyn, I'm because of start here today." He snaps his fingers and moves to lift the ledge up and waves me through.

"Obviously, you're early come through I'll get you a polo. Emily's the associate supervisor, she will prepare you around evening time. She isn't here yet." I finish him to a little office where he starts scrounging through some stockpiling compartments in one of the corners. After a second he jabs his head up and investigates at me "what size?"

"Little will be incredible much obliged." He tosses a shirt at me and focuses me the overall way of the ladies' restroom where I change. Before I leave I require one moment to give myself a quick overview in the full-length reflect on the rear of the entryway. I haven't changed since venturing out from home, my hair actually tumbles to my shoulders in profound earthy colored twists, my eyes are as yet a rich earthy colored tone and my skin is tanned gratitude to my Puerto Rican legacy.

I take a full breath and run my fingers through my hair, my hand on the entryway pulls it open and I stroll once more into the shop with another certainty. I avoid the counter, not exactly accepting the scene before me. The inconsiderate blonde from earlier today is remaining behind the counter, her hair still in a similar muddled bun from toward the beginning of today yet she's changed into a khaki hued shirt, the sleeves moved up to her elbows, uncovering conditioned arms and a little tattoo outwardly of her wrist. The principle contrast in her appearance from today is the grin that is all over, she's chuckling with built person about something and I'm out of nowhere desirous that it isn't me that is making her grin that way. It's very stunning.

I step advances to the counter and make a sound as if to speak, the subsequent her eyes lay on me the grin evaporates, and her eyes enlarge "you must mess with me?" She shouts, her eyebrows nearly vanishing into her hairline.

Unfazed, I venture behind the counter and hold my hand out "we began in an unfavorable mindset prior, I'm Kaitlyn." She hesitantly grasps my hand and I discover I'm the person who pulls away first, the abrupt shock I feel course through my palm stuns me and takes the breeze out of me.

"Emily, look I'm not here to watch so you have a decision. Catch on quickly or stop. It will get occupied later on the grounds that we have an open house for verse readings." I idiosyncrasy and eyebrow being referred to what in particular she's colloquialism making her tighten her lips prior to proceeding "I realize you have barista experience, so I anticipate a great deal."

I need to advise her to remove the stick from her butt since I'm making espresso for understudies on the lowest pay permitted by law. Yet, indeed her quality takes the words out of me and I end up remaining there flickering at her like a device. She feigns exacerbation at me and spots her hands on my shoulders to turn me towards the till. I harden at her straightforward signal, on the grounds that again I feel like 1,000 minuscule electric heartbeats are flying through my body from the spot where her hands rest. "This is the till, press the catch that has the beverages name on and take the cash. It's that basic, figure you can deal with that?"
I go to confront her and tight my eyes marginally "I don't have the foggiest idea, I'm somewhat complimented you expect I can peruse? That is to say, I was trusting there'd be pictures or something." This acquires me a giggle from the person I initially addressed, I definitely should discover what he's called.

"I believe I will like this one Em..." Emily frowns at him and he holds his hands up tragically "and on that note, I'm off. Hot date around evening time." He gestures towards the brunette he was playing with previously and tosses a wink my direction. "Have a decent night women."

I wish his passing supposition had any similarity to truth, yet time hauls. Emily causes me to feel awkward the second only we're. I attempt a few times to initiate discussion with her, each time she either leaves like I haven't spoken at all or she offers me a pitiful response that destroys the endeavor totally. Fortunately it gets occupied and I'm before long put through a lot of hardship, I'm quietly satisfied as far as concerns me time work during secondary school for giving me the experience so now I'm ready to produce lattes, cappuccinos and coffees at a decent speed. I get Emily watching me work from time to time and I feel my face flush, however I drive away any wayward contemplations I get, simply down to the way that she's an awful individual.

When we've shut for the evening and we're preparing to leave I don't think I've ever been so satisfied to leave a spot more than I did well at this point. Be that as it may, it appears for what feels like the millionth time this evening, Emily astonishes me. "Much obliged for this evening Kaitlyn, you surpassed assumptions."

"Jesus, that seems like a school report." I feign exacerbation and watch as she lifts an eyebrow and gets her hands into her pockets "yet much appreciated. I truly am heartbroken about pushing you over prior on... I trust I didn't make you past the point of no return?"

She waves away my conciliatory sentiment and we start strolling through the grounds towards my dormitory building "I responded gravely, I can be... somewhat of an arse." I snicker and fold my arms over my chest, I need to state that is the misrepresentation of reality of the decade. In any case, I reconsider it and stay calm. We keep on strolling peacefully until she stops toward the finish of the road and gives a boisterous murmur "my dormitories along these lines, a debt of gratitude is in order for around evening time. I'll see you around."

I give her a half wave and watch her as she leaves, the swing of her hips is entrancing, and I simply stand and gaze until she adjusts a corner and vanishes from my view. I moan noisily and proceed on my joyful way, feeling a little better when Emily by and by plagues my contemplations. Turns out there might be a smidgen of fairness in her all things considered.

At the point when I make it back to my residence Clara's no place to be seen. What's more, for once, I'm quietly satisfied not to see the particular little redhead. I need to coordinate my considerations about a specific Brit. Hurling myself down on my bed I take a profound moan and endeavor to classify the contemplations I've been having throughout the day. The realities are this; Emily is just dazzling, she's likewise discourteous. She has an amazing grin, however she's very aloof. There was an interesting little flash between us when I shook her hand, and afterward again when she put her hands on my shoulder. I keep thinking about whether she felt it? In the event that she did she made no tendency that she did as such obviously, it's likely uneven. Fuck.

I moan for all to hear and maneuver a cushion onto my chest and catch it to me hard, I'm going to begin saying "poor me" for all to hear while I fall into a spiraling pit of adolescent tension when my flat mate appears at the ideal second and checks out my misery.

"I take it turned out poorly at that point?" She asks, I lift my head to see her raising an eyebrow at me as she disregards her knapsack and drops it onto her work area seat. I moan uproariously and let my head flop back onto the bed.

"It did, yet she was there. The young lady I ran into before."

"Goodness poo, did she say anything?"

"She said parts, turns out she's my chief. Well one of them" I hear Clara let out a low whistle.

"I might not want to be you right now my companion." I moan again prior to propping myself up on my elbows. Taking a gander at her distinctly, I tight my eyes at her and press together my lips.

"Truly? That is all you need to state on the issue? That you wouldn't prefer to be me? Jesus! I would even prefer not to be me at this moment. That is to say, I run into this young lady. Who's exquisite incidentally? She rips my head off, I at that point go through the whole day considering this young lady and afterward similarly as I'm moving beyond the way that I most likely won't see her once more. Turns out I work with her, she's as yet an ass. In any case, Jesus. At the point when she grins, or when she contacts me, I just... I can't even" I flop back and gaze at the roof fan over my bed "I'm disgraceful."

Clara remains calm for a couple of moments; the room is loaded up with the hints of our relaxing. I'm starting to believe she's nodded off when she at long last speaks "Kait, don't whip yourself. That is to say, you simply believe she's hot? That is totally ordinary."

"I surmise so." I state nothing else. I prepare for bed peacefully and tune in as Clara moves around the room and subsides into bed herself. She's snoozing some time before I figure out how to float off and by and by I start considering Emily. Of that short second when I got a fast look into who she truly is, I think I preferred that individual. At the point when I at last nod off my fantasies are brimming with green eyes and winning grins.

Chapter two: You might be correct.

The accompanying not many months pass suddenly, Emily keeps on acting distant with me however I actually get looks into the individual she truly is in the brief minutes where she isn't acting like a dick.

Classes take up my a large portion of my time and when I'm not considering or practicing, I'm working. Returning home for Thanksgiving is a beautiful split away from my overwhelming timetable. I'm irritated at myself for contemplating Emily the whole time I'm away, and it alarms me a little when my heart beat increments when I see her once more. She really grins at me when I start my first move back subsequent to Thanksgiving "great break?"

I gesture as I tie my cover on and leave to clear tables flagging the finish of that short discussion. Being around her actually frightens me, during calm periods at work she sits on a high stool toward the finish of the counter and studies. I asked once what she studies and unexpectedly since meeting her she really chipped in some close to home data "I'm pre-prescription, I graduate this year and afterward off to drug school to complete there" and that brought a dramatic end to that discussion.

Nonetheless, something unusual happened when I was because of return home for Christmas and New year, halfway through my last move before I head off to get my trip down to Texas. Emily began work, I grin at her as she strolls behind the counter and rather than the mandatory grin I've become used to from her she simply glowers and stalks off into the workplace, hammering the entryway behind her. I look across at Zack, built up person, and give him a 'what the hell?' sort of look. He simply shrugs his shoulders and continues to wipe down the tables while I stock up the ice chests.

Emily at last shows up whenever Zack's timed off and we get a surge of understudies coming in for their caffeine fix. She unmistakably isn't satisfied by the aggravation, if looks could execute I think I'd be fallen over on the floor in the wake of being forced to bear the cold glare she fixes me with. "You realize Kaitlyn, I thought you'd have the option to adapt to a couple of espressos. Unmistakably I wasn't right." She lashes out at me after she hands the beverage to the last individual pausing.

I actually don't have the foggiest idea why I picked that evening to snap back, I think my understanding had quite recently worn ragged following quite a while of her blowing sweltering and cold at me. Occasionally she'd address me like I was human, however more often than not she'd overlook me or address me like poo. "You understand what Emily?" I snap at her, my head whipping round to set her with a hard gaze "my poo limits approaching full with you. What the heck is your concern?"

"My concern is that you battle with the most fundamental of errands without requiring some assistance. Advise me, are they all as thick as you where you come from? Or on the other hand would you say you are only an extraordinary sort of country person?"

I saw red at that remark, my jaw fixed and I really held my clench hands at her words. Neither of us were yelling however we had started to draw in inquisitive gazes from the clients that had decided to sit in the bistro and make the most of their beverages. "I don't have a clue the amount more I can take of this. Truth be told," I stop and loosen my cover and toss it down at her feet "take this, and push it up your butt. I imagine that stand up there may be getting somewhat desolate." Before she can say whatever else I push past her difficult to get into the back to recover my things. I need to finish this before I lose face and attempt and take it back. I need this work, however not at the expense of my dignity.

A hand on my arm leaves me speechless, that recognizable shiver I get at whatever point Emily contacts me transmits through my body from that one spot of contact. I let out the breath I'm holding in an insecure murmur and go gradually to take a gander at her. Her demeanor has mollified and she looks practically contrite, I grasp my teeth and fold my arms over my chest insubordinately. We remain there taking a gander at one another peacefully for a couple of seconds, her green eyes looking through my face before she at long last talked. Running a hand through her sandy blonde locks she drops her look and takes a gander at something on the floor "I'm heartbroken." I gesture however put forth no attempt to move "I've had some crap news today and I'm taking it out on some unacceptable individual."

I shrug my shoulders trying to be casual yet inside my nerves are all over from her nearness. "Emily, it's not my business and I don't intend to pry however on the off chance that you need to talk. I'm glad to tune in?" I watch her bite on her base lip and gesture at me. In a move so fast it slows down me a little she walks back out to the counter and raises her voice to get the groups consideration.

"We're shutting early. You have two minutes to drink your beverages or I'm going to sink them." She turns around to me and gives me my cover "help me close down, and afterward we'll talk. On the off chance that you actually need to stop after, well my misfortune I surmise" she streaks me an unbalanced smile and I feel my breath get in my chest.

"Fine." I grab the cover out of her hands and I hear her laugh at me as I mishandle to get it back on. Together, we work peacefully to shut down the shop. We're forced to bear a couple of unsettled protests however Emily in an extremely British and exceptionally considerate manner advised them to quiet the fuck down and disappear. When we've cleaned everything down and she's bolted the front entryways, adequately bolting us inside, butterflies have well and genuinely burned-through my whole internal parts.

She motions to one of the snugs in a corner and we sit down inverse one another, I watch as she pauses for a minute and folds her legs. Her hands squirm in her lap and her temples are weaved in a tight line over her eyes "you know" I start and she gazes toward me "you will give yourself wrinkles on the off chance that you continue to grimace that way."

She chuckles dryly and grins feebly at me "my sweetheart was intended to be flying out for Christmas." My heart stops in my chest at the notice of a sweetheart I had no clue existed. Two contemplations fly through my brain around then; one - she's into young ladies. Two - she's much more inaccessible than she was a moment prior.

I bite my lip briefly as I consider what she's simply said "and I'm speculating because of your foul state of mind that is not happening any longer?"

"Fundamentally. Obviously somethings come up that just can hardly wait, something more significant." She jeers and runs her hands through her hair once more "you know, we've been together since we were sixteen? That is six years together nearly and she's presumably quite possibly the most egotistical individuals I've ever had the setback of knowing." That assertion confounds me and it should peruse clear all over in light of the fact that she smiles at me and chuckles dryly "I understand what you will inquire. For what reason do I stay with her?"

"Practically, however I'm expecting the typical nonexclusive bologna answer. Since you love her?" Admittedly I sound incredibly snarky with my answer, however she doesn't snap back. She takes a gander at me timidly and shrugs her shoulders.

"She wasn't generally similar to this. We've had our high points and low points, when I settled on the decision to concentrate here we chose to separate. We went through the late spring that year going around Europe together and it was, mystical. We didn't contend once, truth be told I'm almost certain I became hopelessly enamored with her once more. We wound up remaining together, we talk day by day and I get over yonder as frequently as could reasonably be expected and the other way around. In any case, she doesn't generally finish her arrangements. Some of the time things she considers more significant come up."

"What could be a higher priority than seeing you?" Smooth. "That is to say, what does she believe is more significant?" Well covered... kinda.

Emily smiles at me as she eccentricities a forehead and folds her hands in her lap "she's a theater understudy. Needs to be on the West End. Generally nibbled parts come up and she gets offered them and I generally get a similar forget about bologna 'this could be the one sweetheart' tsk" she looks neutral and movements in her seat somewhat. "Thus, that basically brings me round trip. Sweetheart was intended to be coming, isn't currently. So I'm currently adhered attempting to discover a trip back to London so I'm not taken off alone." Shit, flights. I check the time and frown.

"I truly don't intend to stop this however I have a trip to get or my mother will convey a lynch horde." This acquires me a snicker from the lady sat opposite me and her eyes meet mine. For that one second the air around us changes, something between us changes. The air among us charges, getting thick to the fact it's practically difficult to relax. I swallow and chomp down on my base lip before she turns her head to turn away and makes a sound as if to speak.

"The least I can do is give you a lift, you've allowed me to bite your ear off for a considerable length of time."

The vehicle ride there is quiet, I continue getting Emily investigating at me and turning away culpably. I can't battle the little rush that shoots through me each time I get one of her transient looks. The air in the vehicle is as yet charged, it's practically unmistakable as it transmits among us. At the point when she pulls up at the drop off point at JFK I go to her and grin bashfully "much obliged for the ride. You truly didn't need to do that."

The manner in which she grins at me is blinding and I feel my heart start to race "genuinely Kaitlyn, it was the least I could do." I stay there simply watching her briefly and afterward I'm abruptly hit with a motivation I realize I will kick myself for some other time.

"Give me your telephone." I hold my hand out and she sees me confounded.

"Why?"

"Since I'm furtively expecting to locate a bare picture or two." Rolling my eyes I get her slight redden and smile "I will give you my number. In the event that poop goes down and you need to talk, you can call. Or then again text. Whatever suits you." Emily gives me her telephone with anxiety painted clear all over "and in case I'm being straightforward I could utilize the interruption, my folks make me crazy." This acquires me a giggle and I smile at her, she has a lovely, joyful snicker. I give careful consideration to attempt to make her chuckle more later on to make sure I can hear that stunning sound.

"Fine, have a protected flight." Once again we locate each other to gazing at one another so I accomplish something different totally without much forethought, something that I will go through the following three weeks considering fanatically. I lean forward and kiss her cheek delicately, when I pull away Emily's eyes are wide and her hand is laying on her cheek in the spot where I kissed her. It's dim inside the vehicle however the become flushed on her cheek is unmissable, I'm additionally certain that my heart could be heard beating ceaselessly some place in Alaska it was pulsating so noisily.

"Have a decent Christmas Em..." I mumble as my hand stops on the entryway handle.

"You too, Kait."

***

At the point when I get back from winter break I have a wonderful skip in my progression and a glad tune all the rage. Christmas had been a fascinating illicit relationship, sure seeing my family was pleasant. In any case, it was the every day messaging spells with Emily that had me in a particularly positive state of mind as I wind up on my first run since being once again at school.

When you work on that super cold disposition there's a very entertaining, keen and child lady simply shouting to be taken note. Allowed each time she disclosed to me she was spending time with Charlotte I'd fume with an unburdened desire. In any case, at that point something would come up and the messaging with proceed and usually I'd nod off with the greatest grin all over.

Our last experience has been circling in my psyche on rehash, playing again and again. I consider all that we stated, the manner in which the air around us charged and a gleam of expectation would light within me that I rushed to drench.

The music in my ears was giving a soundtrack to the musicality of my feet on the walkway, I have my head down and I am running for all it is worth. The January air chomps my cheeks, ears and nose however the remainder of my body consumes the effort. Adjusting a corner toward my dormitory I stop suddenly to abstaining from impacting straight into a clueless passerby. "Oh my goodness, nearly!" I shout before I get a decent gander at the individual before me. Remaining before me is Emily with a smile all the rage and one of her ideal temples quirked. I haul my earphones out and set her with a grin "we need to quit running into one another like this, individuals will undoubtedly begin talking."

She chuckles, that breathtaking ringer like snicker, the sort of giggle that makes my heart grip with euphoria to hear it "let them, you need to begin watching where you're going" I wave her off and take a long beverage from my water bottle "great Christmas?" I idiosyncrasy an eyebrow at her and rooster my head aside, she realizes how my Christmas was, we'd burned through its majority talking.

"It was alright, my sisters were done with their children and individual spouses so the house was insane, got hauled to mass a couple of times. Yet, it was ideal to see everybody. You?"

"Would be advised to" She grins at me and shrugs her shoulders "found my sibling, saw Charlotte, figured out how to piss my mum off. Yet, that is not actually anything new." The notice of her better half in a split second sets me anxious and I start searching for a reason to leave, to leave this discussion. I check the time and recoil a bit.

"Crap is that the time? I have class in an hour and I need to shower" I stroll around her and go to make a couple of strides in reverse "look up some other time?"

Emily looks befuddled yet holds that perfect grin all over "OK, it was acceptable seeing you Kait."

I gesture accordingly and dismiss to run the overall way of my dormitory Catalina Suarez, you are a screwing moron! Seeing Emily again feels mixed nearly, it's totally obvious to me that I'm insane for her however there's the always present sweetheart approaching over me. I shouldn't allow myself to consider her that way, particularly when I realize I can't have her the manner in which I need. How is it you need her Suarez? Gracious, I'd have her in any case she'd let me!

Nothing can occur, I need to grapple with that. However, that doesn't mean I can't be her companion? Isn't that right?

***

The coming weeks pass pretty gradually, my captivation by Emily doesn't wind down on the off chance that anything it deteriorates. Presently when we're on move together we really talk, not all that much however things are significantly more loose than they used to be and I start seeing an alternate side to her. Which doesn't make my pound any simpler to fail to remember.

At some point towards the finish of March I some way or another figure out how to be elected to finish the finish of quarter stock check with her. Which energizes me more than it ought to, three hours of continuous time with Emily? What's not to cherish?

We work peacefully for some time, I wind up taking secret ganders at her jean clad legs, really valuing the manner in which the blue denim tightens in at her hips and embraces her thighs like a subsequent skin. She has a plaid shirt on that creeps up at whatever point she comes to up to one of the higher racks, uncovering a smooth, conditioned stomach that makes my mouth dry. In any case, as much as I love looking at my blonde companion, the work is dreary and following an hour or so I discover my fixation melting away.

With a boisterous murmur I bow on the floor to start checking the containers of mineral water kept on one of the base racks "estoy tan aburrido."

Emily goes to grin at me "deja de quejarte y sigue con eso."

My mouth nearly hits the floor when I hear her answer to me in Spanish "you communicate in Spanish?" I denounce boisterously, this makes her laugh dryly and she shrugs her shoulders coolly.

"I had costly training."

"Care to expound?" I counter, she can be so harsh some of the time however I'm fixated on learning any data she will give to more readily splash a portion of the secret that encompasses this lady. Perhaps then I can quit fixating on her.

I tune in as Emily takes a full breath and see her run her hands through her hair "my folks, well my Mum more than Dad, sent my sibling and I to tuition based schools. Truly outstanding in the nation, extremely restrictive, over the top expensive."

"Sort of like Hogwarts?" I joke, and relish the manner in which her giggle sounds out in the unfilled shop.

"Assuming just, no it was extremely vainglorious. I loathed it did as well, Max. Be that as it may, I had no way out, I was made to get familiar with an instrument and go to move classes and do all the things a 'woman' ought to do as my mom would state. She abhorred that my Dad would take me and Maxie to football at the end of the week, that is soccer to you lesser society."

I chicken an eyebrow and overlay my arms over my chest "you know, one day you will make a joke to our detriment and do it to some unacceptable individual. Plus, in light of the fact that I was brought into the world in Texas doesn't make me American. I'm pleased with my Puerto Rican legacy."

"Bravo" she winks at me and my heart stops briefly "back to my story now" I feign exacerbation and return to including the things before me "working up to my high schooler years, soon after my folks separated, I revolted a bit. My Dad has consistently been significantly more laid back than my mom, she

29

constrained me to gain proficiency with an instrument. For a year I played the pack pipes just to irritate her. She set some hard boundaries and marked me up for piano exercises at life experience school, I was additionally shipped off to move class as a child."

"So with everything taken into account you were a legitimate little woman? What the heck occurred?" I kidded.

"I grew up I presume. I began investing more energy at dad's, didn't address mum except if it was essential. At the point when I came out, oh my goodness. She hit the rooftop. Father was flawless about it, disclosed to me he wasn't amazed. He's constantly been benevolent to Charlotte, regardless of whether he thinks I merit better."

"Well I can't actually remark on that, what made you come right to America to consider?" I ask, really inquisitive.

She laughs somewhat and loosens up to a high rack, cutting down a case of product to check and giving me an awful perspective on her stomach "well I surmise that was another immense screw you to my mom. She's a specialist, she works in a nearby specialists practice and needed my sibling and I to emulate her example. Just issue is Maxie went into law and works with my father. I've for the longest time been itching to be a specialist however I would prefer not to go into general practice in the UK. I need to be a specialist, so that is the thing that I'm doing. I know if I somehow managed to do this in England she'd go through the following eight years meddling while I experience college and the remainder of it. Be that as it may, over here I'm in charge. I picked New York, all being admirably I'll be going to Harvard for drug school and afterward into a decent residency program." The track on Emily's iPod changes similarly as she completes the process of talking and she takes a gander at me with a fiendish flicker in her eyes "I love this melody, mind in the event that I turn it up?"

"Pull out all the stops." She wrenches up the volume and a rowdy melody I don't perceive starts playing, I'm delighted to see her dance somewhat on the spot. Remaining from my position I move to the beverages refrigerator around the counter, my consideration is before long turned somewhere else when I hear Emily start to sing.

I investigate and watch her watching me, a little grin all the rage "Friday night I dropped in on your gathering, Saturday I said I'm grieved, Sunday came and destroyed me out once more. I was just having a good time, wasn't harming anybody and we as a whole delighted in the end of the week for a change" I characteristic my eyebrow at her, my cheeks heat somewhat however I turn my consideration back to the job that needs to be

31

done. Tragically for me I don't hear her sneak up on me when the tune starts "you might be correct, I might be insane" alarmed, I pivot and see her standing a foot or so away, her entire body moving in a cheerful route to the music. "Be that as it may, it just might be an insane person no doubt about it!" I raise an eyebrow and shake my head at her.

An energetic grin contacts my lips as I watch her dance around briefly, when she gets my attention again she stops and puts her hands on her hips "what's so entertaining?"

Shrugging my shoulder, I cockerel my head and respect her cautiously "nothing, I'm simply pondering where it's gone is all."

She sees me baffled briefly, her foreheads wrinkling and her lips fixing somewhat "where what's no more?"

"The stick that appears to forever dwell up your rear end. It has all the earmarks of being missing."

Emily stands frozen in place briefly and watches me cautiously briefly, briefly I start to feel frustrated about what I said. I would not like to hope for the best with her however she normally makes the most of my comical inclination. My concerns are fleeting however as she before long beginnings giggling hard "reasonable remark Suarez. Billy Joel is a mystery love of mine.

Not humiliated. Indeed, most likely not as much as I ought to be in any case." She finished that with another wink and it took all my won't to dissolve into an estrogen filled puddle not too far off on the floor.

Heading out in different directions that night was a tragic undertaking for me, Emily had been a delight to associate with the entire evening. Telling wisecracks, offering bits of knowledge to who she is, getting some information about my family. When I returned to my room I was grinning ear to ear, a silly smile solidly planted on my highlights.

"I take it work was pleasant?" My instinctive companion asked as I inclined toward the shut way to our shared room and moaned like an adoration wiped out youngster. I rushed to scowl at her as I felt my chest fixing, the full power of my emotions felt like they could suffocate me whenever and as usual, I felt silly when I considered exactly how terrible I had it for my newly discovered English companion.

"It was, I'm a screwing imbecile." I said with a miserable tone, moving over to my bed I sit on the edge and grasp my head "what am I doing Clara?" I can feel the tears consuming in my eyes, taking steps to gush out. My chest feels weighty as I'm hit with the truth of what's happening. This lady, this wonderful, baffling lady has dazzled me and she's inaccessible. I need her so terrible and I can't have her, not that I'd actually have the option to have her in any case. "I'm such a screwing masochist."

Clara moves from her bed and I feel the sleeping cushion plunge as she plunks down close to me, her arm wraps around my shoulders as she endeavors to comfort me. "You have it for her quite awful eh?"

I gaze upward and gaze at her, my temples sewed firmly, I squint hard for a couple of seconds attempting my hardest to stop the tears that are taking steps to gush out over from breaking liberated from my eyes "you have no clue."

Chapter three: That's what companions are for

Emily and I end up turning out to be dear companions as the semester draws on. Over and over we see each other outside of work, we started running together, going out for espresso or to the films. My fixation on her hadn't gone, the additional time I go through with her the more I wind up falling further, falling more enthusiastically, soon she resembles oxygen. I can't envision not having her around, so being the insatiable, masochistic child of bitch that I am, I take what I can get. Furthermore, if that is simply companionship, all things considered, I surmise that should do.

Approaching the finish of the semester I wind up in an off-kilter position, a piece of my last grade incorporates orchestrating and coordinating a brief melodic number. I picked my performers, my artists, idealized the plans and was certain that I planned to spend my first year with a strong evaluation.

That was until my piano player caught an instance of the mumps three days before we were opened in to perform and be evaluated. "You're simply must play Kait" Chloe said as she paced the practice space.

"How the fuck would i be able to guide you part from behind a piano?" I snap back at her, running my fingers through my newly cut, short earthy colored locks.

Chloe glares back at me and folds her arms over her chest disobediently "I don't have the foggiest idea. However, YOU need to fix this. I will get espresso." That's when motivation hit me, I know it's a since quite a while ago shot however as the difficult blonde avoids the room I fish my mobile phone with regards to my handbag and dial a number with shaking fingers.

The individual gets after three rings and I inhale a murmur of alleviation "Emily, hello it's Kaitlyn."

"Sort of figured, I have this mystically thing called a guest show."

"Ha, you know you're adorable when you attempt to be amusing yet I'm in a jam and I need some help." I bite my lip and speed in a little circle, procuring some sketchy looks from my schoolmates .

"Shoot."

"You play piano right?"

"Erm, it's been some time yet definitely why?" Comes the answer, Emily sounds questionable and I wind up biting my base lip, my hand moves to my hair and I start whirling a lock apprehensively between my fingers.

"I wouldn't inquire as to whether I wasn't frantic however my last grade relies upon this, I need somebody to step in for my piano player. He's become sick short notification. I'd do it, before you state anything, however I can't immediate from behind a piano."

I can hear Emily moan through the handset and I don't understand I'm holding my breath until I hear her talk again and let it out in a long murmur "I surmise so. In any case, you owe me. Where and when?"

"Expressions of the human experience building, drop me a book when you arrive and I'll meet you outside." Emily detaches without saying bye and I go to the gathering sitting, gazing at me "I've arranged it. Begin doing your warmups. When Chloe and Emily arrive we'll get to it." Without hanging tight for an answer I leave the room and continue to stroll to the outside of the structure to sit on the low divider covering the walkway to the front passage.

I realize I said I'd hang tight for her call however truth be told I'm overjoyed at the possibility of her dropping everything to come and help me. She has a sweetheart... I shake away my snarky internal musings and cast my look down to the walkway underneath my feet. Shaking my leg in anxious expectation I lose myself to my musings, however I'm prepared for seeing her. I just saw her last night however in the couple of hours where I wasn't in her organization , missed her.

When I feel a couple of cool hands slip over my eyes, I don't frighten I smile broadly and begin chuckling "think about who?"

"Megan Fox, you've at last woken up and acknowledged I'm the lone lady for you?"

Emily eliminates her hands from my face and sits close to me on the divider, poking me with her shoulder "you're unpleasant. You trim your hair?" She asks connecting with one of her long sensitive fingers to pull on an unpredictable twist prior to allowing it to fall free once more.

"Either that or it contracted in the shower." I comment, poking her with my shoulder. Her eyes get mine and they lock together briefly. I could become mixed up in her eyes and carry on with a glad life there.

Emily starts to smile broadly at me and shakes her head somewhat "your mockery is reviving Kait" her teeth stress her base lip as we sit unobtrusively before she talks once more "things being what they are, you need my assistance?"

I lay my head on her shoulder and gesture "that's right, and you're a lifeline. Much obliged to you." I take in her sublime fragrance and close my eyes briefly, savoring her closeness before I need to isolate myself.

"Whenever Kait, will we get to it?" I remain at her words and gesture, she goes with the same pattern and we walk together to the practice space I've involved. "What is it I will play? I ought to caution you I'm clumsy."

"I've orchestrated a Disney mixture. There's some astonishing performers and it was the lone thing I could get them to concur on. It's a blend between melodies sung by saints and scoundrels. Took me always, yet so far I've been content with the outcomes." I understand I'm spouting and stop suddenly, my cheeks flaring marginally.

"Sounds great. Well as long as there's sheet music I ought to have the option to wade through."

In the practice room I present Emily momentarily, clarifying that she isn't a music understudy. Truth be told when I tell the gathering that she's a pre-medications senior they all look somewhat awestruck. I look over at my light haired companion and see her smiling, guiding her to the piano she sits down and the remainder of the performers take their places. "Alright, so all of you understand what you're doing. So we'll take it from the earliest starting point. Emily, you're content with the key changes I've noted yes?" I look behind me and discover her watching me intently.

"Of course, it may take a few times to hit the nail on the head yet I think I'll arrive." I smile at her and flush when she winks at me my goodness, for what reason does she need to do that?

I make a sound as if to speak and get some distance from her, raising my arms I include them and they start playing. Emily's acceptable, indeed, she's magnificent. I hazard looks across at her and watch her hands fly carefully over the keys, the muscles in her arms moving in time with the music. The sight alone is sufficient to light starts of excitement somewhere down in my gut, I could remain here and watch her throughout the day. Her simple effortlessness, the manner in which her foreheads wrinkle into a tight line over her eyes, I've had lady friends previously, had pulverizes yet nothing like this. She never neglects to hypnotize me.

As the tune reaches a conclusion I grin at the room before me and get the heap of papers on the work area "that was extraordinary, how about we take five and go once more." I need to go address Emily however I sharp pull on the rear of my sweatshirt leaves me speechless, investigating my shoulder I see Chloe giving me a careful look.

"Outside. Presently." I look behind me at Emily who's watching me in disarray, offering her a little, conciliatory grin I obediently follow Chloe to the passage outside the study hall. "Who's that and what is she to you?" Straight forthright not surprisingly, I run my hand through my short bolts and shrug my shoulders.

"She's Emily, we cooperate. We're simply companion why?" I attempt and keep my voice even, I would prefer not to show how I really feel about her. Chloe, being the reckless, natural young lady I've come to know simply idiosyncrasies a blonde eyebrow at me and goads me in the chest.

"Try not to horse crap me Kaitlyn, I saw the manner in which you took a gander at her. You like her don't you?" My teeth start to stress my lower lip as I watch Chloe watching me cautiously. I peer through the open entryway we've quite recently come through and get Emily taking a gander at me, she grins energetically and mouths 'you alright?' from across the room.

I gesture my answer and glance back at Chloe "definitely, yet nothing will actually occur. She's taken and we're simply companions." The look I receive consequently from Chloe is one I don't need, she takes a gander at me in a miserable way "don't see me like that. I don't need your pity." I snap, glaring back at her.

Chloe connects and contacts my arm delicately "I don't feel sorry for you Kait, simply be cautious." I gesture and dismiss, apprehensive that my feelings will improve of me on the off chance that I dive any further into this discussion. I scorn considering all the things I need with Emily in light of the fact that I realize they won't occur. I need to proceed onward, meet a decent young lady and date her. However, every time I draw near to that I wind up contrasting them with my English companion and they fail to measure up.

The remainder of the meeting flies by and I end up sitting close to Emily at the piano in the now unfilled room. The stool is sufficiently wide to fit both of us however it implies the sides of our bodies are contacting, which never really quiet the butterflies in my stomach. "You play superbly" I comment as her fingers tinker with the ivory keys, she halts abruptly and takes a gander at me with a naughty flicker in her eye.

"Your chance to show me what you can do I think" she comments, I'm not scared of the test having been playing since I was six. I'm very acceptable. I simply shrug my shoulders, the development making my arm rub against her and start playing the launch of Clare de Lune yet battle to arrive at the higher notes without extending across her body. This isn't unwanted yet being so near her consistently makes intelligent thoroughly considering go the window.

I stop suddenly and go to see her ideal face "I figure you should play with me" that acquires me a quirked forehead and a grin, tuning in back to what exactly I've said I turn beet red and make snappy to correct what I've quite recently said "I mean the piano... not that you should play with me myself since you know... that would be wrong and... poo." Emily's watching me in entertainment while I bunch screw my way through this suggestion.

"Kaitlyn?"

"That's right?"

"Quit talking, how about we go eat. Your treat." I gesture quietly and permit her to lead me out of the room, together we stroll peacefully to one of the off grounds bars. Neither of us speak, I don't have the foggiest idea what I'm intended to state to her in the wake of having made a genuine imbecile out of myself. How can it be that at whatever point I'm around her I can scarcely bungle through a full discussion?

We sit opposite one another at a table towards the rear of the bar "thank you for now, ideally Simon ought to be back when we're booked to play however in the event that not would you mind stepping in once more?"

"Obviously, just let me know. There are a few talks I can't miss this week however after that I'm simply packing for finals." The typical pity that flows through me is exactly on schedule when Emily raises her unavoidable graduation, which means she'll be leaving to head out to Medical School in Connecticut "everything alright Kait? You've been more bizarre than common today."

I feign exacerbation at her correspond however bite on my base lip, do I come clean with her? Reveal to her that I'm besotted by her and that I don't need her to leave or do I skate past that theme and horse crap her obviously "I'm fine, only dismal to consider the reality you'll be leaving soon." Mostly evident, however not every bit of relevant information. Emily takes a gander at me for what feels like quite a while, she makes no sign that she's going to state anything. After a second she connects across the table and places her hand on top of mine, my eyes eat up to meet hers and by and by that charge is there. That pull I feel attracting me to her is there once more, my body emanates with an electric flow where her hand contacts mine. Absent a lot of thought or respect for outcomes I ribbon my fingers through hers and run my thumb across the rear of her hand, I anticipate that her should grab her hand away, breaking the spell between us. However, she doesn't, she crushes my hand more tight. "Do you feel it?" The words sneak out of me softly however my eyes stay on hers, I watch as she holds her jaw and shuts her eyes before she gestures gradually.

When her eyes open again they have a removed look in them, she doesn't grab her hand away yet she looks practically irate? "I do Kait, yet I can't." Rejected, I start to pull my hand away yet she simply holds it more tight "don't. If you don't mind Just..." She runs her fingers through her hair with her free hand "allow me one more moment like this?" I simply gesture and drop my other hand to cover hers.

"Anything..." it comes out as right around a murmur however in this little trade that happens between us something becomes exposed for me, something that the two makes my heart skip with happiness and makes it break simply somewhat more. Emily knows how I feel about her and obviously quite possibly's she feels a similar way. However, she's recognized that regardless of whether she feels something she can't. In couple of words she's made it plentifully certain that nothing will actually occur.

Emily ultimately slips her hand out of mine and glimmers me a timid grin and we request our food. We eat together and talk like we generally would, both quietly consenting to disregard the second we've recently shared. I thought Emily was acceptable at veiling her feelings, anyway on the stroll back to our quarters she gets me by my coat sleeve and pulls me to a stop so I'm stood straightforwardly before her. Her inebriating aroma overpowers every one of my faculties, I gaze toward her through my eyelashes, watching her watch me eagerly with those excellent green eyes.

My breathing stops unexpectedly when I feel her run her fingertips down the length of my cheek gradually, her eyes never leaving mine. My hands discover their way to her hips and I rest them there delicately, the air encompassing us pops with force as we remain there taking a gander at one another, our countenances so close I can feel the glow of her breath on my skin as I lean my face excitedly into her touch. My entire body knows about that basic stroke against my cheek, my knees clasp somewhat when she runs her thumb along my base lip and my covers ripple shut fully expecting her kiss. "I need to Kaitlyn, I truly need to. However, I can't." Emily's sounds tormented when she talks, breaking the quiet spell between us. I gesture my agreement, tears consuming in my eyes as the sinking feeling settles over me when I understand she's stinging over this.

My arms drop to my side, prepared to make my flight immediately when Emily cups my face in both of her hands and presses her lips immovably against my temple. I let a little wail get away from my lips at the contact and fold my arms over her midsection "kindly don't cry Kaitlyn..." Emily's voice breaks deceiving her feelings as her arms fall around my shoulders holding me near her.

I've contemplated this for such a long time, about how it would feel to be near her, to have her arms around me. I never needed

46

it to be this agonizing, this hard. It shouldn't be this way "let me go" I state for all to hear, battling out of her arms. Isolating myself from her I swallow in natural air, filling my lungs trying to clear my head. "I don't think you've pondered how hard this is for me Emily, to see you consistently. Knowing how I feel, suspecting how you do and realizing nothing can actually occur?" My voice breaks on the last two words and I take a forming breath prior to proceeding "I realize you have a sweetheart, you never neglect to help me to remember that little truth. In any case, where right? When was the last time she could possibly do whatever was for you and not only for her?" I step forward, seeing her face cautiously "I won't request that you pick since I realize I won't care for your decision. Yet, simply know this," in a move bolder than I believed I twisted my fingers around her jawline and moved her face so she was seeing me "I'd move mountains to be with you and nothing could actually be a higher priority than you or us." I don't utter a word else, nor do I hang tight for her answer.

Pivoting suddenly I walk rapidly back to my apartment, the tears falling unreservedly from my eyes, my appalling and the words I'd recently verbally expressed ringing in my ear.

Chapter four: Sweetest Goodbye

"Hey now Kait, only one date. The schools painting the town for graduates, I have an additional ticket. Accompany me?" Gemma asks me for what feels like the thousandth time, this isn't the first run through she's asked me out. Nor is it the first occasion when I've said no. She's presently inclining toward the counter while I'm working, I feign exacerbation and moan noisily prior to pivoting to take a gander at the lady remaining there.

She's appealing it is extremely unlikely around that, short edited dark hair and penetrating blue eyes. She's an appealing butch, which is extraordinary if that is the thing that you're in to. Her lips are more slender than Emily's nevertheless she's plainly fit as a fiddle. Quit contrasting each lady you meet with her. "When is it?" I ask watching her face nearly split in two from the wide smile that breaks out across her attractive highlights.

"Friday. I could get you at seven?" I bite my base lip, uncertain on where to go from here. I've been passing her over for such a long time, it's a bit of charming that she hasn't recently surrendered at this point. I'm going to disclose to her no again when the chime looming over the front entryway rings, flagging the appearance of another client. Quietly grateful for the respite I've been given to work out how I will deny Gemma, once more, I go to the front counter and my heart stops. Emily is strolling to the counter inseparably with a lady I can just accept that is her better half. More limited than Emily with reflexive, earthy colored hair, the young ladies absolutely excellent and out of nowhere I'm feeling incredibly reluctant. Emily's eyes enlarge when she sees me standing sitting tight for her and her steps abbreviate, as though she needs to dodge the abnormal experience going to occur as much as I do.

Our eyes lock on one another and my breath gets in my throat, my chest fixes as I watch the lady I've pined after for such a long time stop straightforwardly before me and I make an honest effort to not resemble an injured doggy "howdy, what would i be able to get for you?" I keep my welcome brief and forthright, to save myself from saying something I realize I'll lament over the long haul.

Emily eyes me hypothetically briefly, she was unmistakably wanting to think not to see me here today. Indeed we've been doing admirably in dodging each other in the course of the most recent couple of weeks since our nearly kiss and my straightforward admission. I've missed her, there's no alternate method to state it, I've missed everything about her and considering her to be there looking as great as could be expected close to somebody who isn't me just makes that empty pit in my stomach extend "I didn't have any acquaintance with you were working today Kaitlyn" I shrug my shoulders and evade her penetrating look.

"I traded with Zack, he had a class he was unable to miss and I had my last yesterday so I was free." My voice is proficient however obliging as I remain there moving from foot to foot. This isn't off-kilter in any way.

Emily remains there quietly briefly until her better half bumps her, taking her back to the explanation she's remaining there "goodness, apologies. Would we be able to get a cappuccino and a twofold coffee please?"

I gesture and start making their beverages, attempting to abstain from taking a gander at the couple remaining before the counter "are you going to offer me a response at that point?" Gemma's inquiry alarms me, I'd failed to remember she was there yet looking again back at Emily who has her lips to her lady friends ear, presumably murmuring sweet things into it deciding by the little grin playing on the brunette lips. As I take in that little second, it brings a new flood of hurt and blame over me that I demonstration recklessly in the following second.
I go to take a gander at Gemma, a decided look spread across my highlights I gesture "sure, why not. I'm certain I can discover something to wear. I'll see you at that point." Gemma's smile is infectious and I grin back at her momentarily before she writes her cell number down on a napkin and hands it to me.

"Text me your location, I'll meet you there and we can go together." I gesture my arrangement, taking the napkin and watch as Gemma leaves the shop. Hesitantly, I place the two cups before Emily and give her a hardened grin.

Charlotte looks among us and makes a sound as if to speak "sweetheart, are you going to present me?" Emily's eyes don't leave my face as she presents us and I give her better half a polite handshake.

"It's so pleasant to at long last meet you Charlotte, I've heard a great deal about you."

"Similarly Kaitlyn, you're not in any way like I envisioned you'd be" that remark arouses my curiosity and I eccentricity an eyebrow at her.

"Truly? How could you envision me to be?" I ask somewhat more keen than was likely needed.

Emily makes a sound as if to speak and I look back at her momentarily "for what reason don't we take this out with us angel? We can take a stroll before supper?" I turn my back to the couple and occupied myself cleaning down the back counter, I hazard a look behind me when I hear the ringer toll again and watch as they leave connected at the hip.

***

"Alright, so how would I look?" I ask Clara doing a full spin so she can see the dress I've decided to wear. I chose not to purchase anything for the event, appreciative that I have this dark mid-length dress for quite a long time, for example, this. My shoulders are exposed as the material sticks to the highest point of my arms, removing at my elbows, the body of the dress embraces my bends like a subsequent skin and my heels give me some additional tallness. I've left my hair falling in its common twists sitting against the delicate skin of my uncovered shoulders.

Clara looks at me rapidly and whistles in thankfulness "you look hot young lady, however advise me, have you gone to this exertion for your date? Or on the other hand for another senior who you're wanting to chance upon?"

That question finds me napping, Clara knows precisely what happened among Emily and I. I returned home a damn wreck that evening and amazingly she stayed up with me the vast majority of the late evening allowing me to talk and cry until I at last nodded off from sheer fatigue "my date clearly, I revealed to Emily how I felt and she's kept away from me at all costs from that point onward," Clara cuts me off with a look and shakes her head.

"You've been evading her too Kait, don't deny it."

"I have my reasons" I counter rebelliously, checking the advanced clock on my end table I moan and put on some lip sparkle in the mirror. "I would be wise to go, Gemma will be here any moment."

Clara maneuvers me into an embrace "don't do anything moronic. Simply have a good time. She's settled on her decision" holding me at a careful distance she grins heartily at me and after one final waiting look releases me.

Gemma obviously is as of now hanging tight for me outside, and seeing her finds me napping. She looks great wearing what must be a custom-made coat, pants and dress shirt, a light blue tie hanging freely around her neck "Kaitlyn, goodness... you look... goodness" I redden marginally and give her a wily smile.

"Much obliged, you don't look really awful yourself." Gemma rubs the rear of her neck ungracefully and neither of us talks again briefly. She moves towards me and holds her hand out to me, which I go for and we stroll away from my structure together.

"I'm happy you at long last consented to this Kait" I chuckle at this and shrug my shoulders non-committedly prior to reacting.

"You were extremely tireless" I commented prior to bumping her with my shoulder "I am as well, where is this thing at any rate?"

Guiding me towards the parking garage and to her vehicle, Gemma holds open the traveler entryway for me and smiles "they leased the capacity suite at the Hilton, there's free drinks too. Ought to be a goodbye"

The drive to the lodging hushed up, Gemma is an alluring lady, kind and really keen on seeking after something with me. In any case, so far I feel no flash, nothing there that makes me need to give myself wholeheartedly to her and hellfire to the results. Dislike how it is with Emily. I make an effort not to murmur so anyone can hear at my inner clash, I would prefer not to go down that hare opening. No good thing actually comes from it, rather I need to attempt to zero in on the individual I'm here with.

The capacity suite at the inn is brightened delightfully, glimmering lights embellish the dividers and roofs, inflatables, fresh white decorative spreads. It would seem that the

University has gone hard and fast, Gemma has my hand with hers and rapidly drives me over to a table loaded with her companions and presents me. She's mindful enough to haul my seat out for me prior to taking the one to one side and hanging an arm across the rear of my seat, her fingers finding a spot at the rear of one of my shoulders where she starts to stroke the skin systematically.

I quickly worry, knowing in the rear of my brain that I don't need her to contact me. I subdue that idea rapidly, recalling the guarantee I made to myself on the ride over and power my body to unwind. It shows up however that that is the place where Gemma's mindfulness finished, whenever she has sat with her companions and made basic presentations I'm excluded from the discussion. Truth be told, on the off chance that it wasn't her hand contacting me I'd have speculated that she'd failed to remember I was even there.

Tired and exhausted I remain from my seat unexpectedly "pardon me, I'm going to the washroom." I don't sit tight for her reaction prior to leaving, this was a slip-up, I realized I shouldn't have consented to go out with her. I protest to myself as I stroll through the room, staying away from understudies and tables as I go. I fix my eyes to the floor underneath me, similarly as I might suspect I'm away from everybody before I hammer into someone else, nearly thumping us both to the floor. "Oh my goodness, I am so sorry..." I start, halting myself when I see who it is that I've strolled into.

Emily has her hands on my arms steadying us both, as forever her touch beats through my body like an electric flow. "You need to begin focusing on where you're going" she criticizes me, her voice delicate, I notice that she puts forth no attempt to release me. I likewise notice that her eyes are at present going here and there my body ravenously prior to laying all over once more "Kaitlyn," she takes a profound nearly quieting breath "you look wonderful."

I give back in kind and savor her insatiably, being so slippery with her as of late has been troublesome, some of the time I sense that I've failed to remember exactly how delightful she is. So I take a gander at her gradually, my eyes going over her body longingly, drawing her into my mind. She's wearing dull dark pants, a naval force blue dress shirt wrapped up at her hips and a dark vest closed up absurd. Her hair falls in waves, outlining her face "chose to conflict with a dress?" Of the relative multitude of comments I pick that?

Emily smiles, her hands running down my arms until they drop to her side where she pushes them into her pockets "you were unable to pay me enough to put one on. What are you doing here? I thought this was for graduates as it were?"

I moan and gesture towards Gemma "I'm intended to be out on the town however it's a fiasco." I try checking out the room "where's Charlotte?" Emily feigns exacerbation and shakes her head.

"Her representative called and she just needed to take it, so here I am."

I grin at her and gesture "so here you are." I concur, our eyes meet and I can taste the air around us change. It's distinctive to how it typically is, the strain that has been there as of late has proceeded to have been supplanted with an implicit yearning. The music changes and is supplanted by a moderate song being played, I watch as couples around us take to the floor and start influencing together.

Emily removes a hand from its pocket and takes one of mine "this may be off the mark, yet do you think it'd be alright in the event that we moved one time together?" Her voice hushes up, practically confident when she asks me and I can't help the grin that creeps onto my lips.

I press her hand and bit nearer to her "it's not off the mark. I think it'd be more than alright." The manner in which she takes a gander at me before she hauls me to the dance floor and covers us between couples so we're far out makes my knees powerless. At the point when she folds her arms over my midriff in the wake of lifting mine to around her neck, I feel the world dissolve away, her eyes don't leave mine and I soften into the shapes of her body.

She plunges her head and leans her cheek against mine "I'm grieved" she murmurs as we influence together, her arms fix around me like she's worried I'm going to vanish. "I'm grieved that I can't be what you need me to be. I'm sorry I can't be what I need to be, she's moving over here. I can't leave her currently she's settled on that decision."

I gesture gradually, overlooking the burning agony in my chest as she speaks "I see Emily. Try not to apologize, it sucks, for the two of us." I concede, pulling back somewhat so I can see her "doesn't mean you can go off and disregard me however, I mean it when I state I will miss you."

She smiles at me and leans her brow against mine "I'll miss you as well, more than you'll know."

Quietness falls on us and I just let myself appreciate being with her, at that time there's simply us. No ungainliness, no pressure, no sweethearts, just us being together. "What do we do now?" I ask, hesitant to break the harmony between us.

Emily murmurs and presses her lips to my hair delicately "we continue to move, you return to your date, finish school. Be marvelous. I'll proceed to discover Charlotte, go to Harvard and attempt to cover these affections for you."

"Alright." I state as my heart breaks into 1,000,000 little pieces, when the music closes we hesitantly unravel from each other and offer one final passing look. With a shy grin, Emily changes direction suddenly and vanishes from my sight and from my life.

She graduated a couple of days after the fact and even with the guarantee to stay in contact, that was the last I got with her.

Chapter five: After this time.

I disdain emergency clinics, presumably more than I scorn blood and right now I need to bear both gratitude to an idiotic courier bicycle not watching where the screw he was going. So as opposed to being grinding away at the theater, here I am sat in the trauma center at New York: Presbyterian Hospital holding on to get my arm sewed up.

My leg shakes eagerly as I hold the towel onto my arm, it's splashed with warm, tacky blood and it's leaking from the fabric and onto my fingers. The smell sticks in my nose, blending in with the clinical fragrance of blanch sickens me and my stomach annoys at it. I moan noisily when my wireless rings with one more message from my manager asking how I am. I hit fortunate with my entry level position, working underneath extraordinary compared to other Broadway Musical chiefs in the business, in addition to he's a stunning fellow and he and his accomplice have done everything to cause me to feel welcome and regularly blow away what is normal.

It shows up the stand by is over when the drape is pulled back unexpectedly and before me is a bothered looking Doctor "Catalina Suarez? I'm Doctor Emily Forester, I accept you're needing a couple of stitches?" That voice, that name, it seems like an affront when I see the lady remaining before me. It may have been a long time since I last saw her however I'll always remember the sound of that voice, that complement or those puncturing green eyes. I need to speak, I need to state anything besides words get away from me as I gaze into those eyes I investigated so regularly every one of those years back. Be that as it may, the power of the yearning I felt hits me with a similar power of a cargo train and delivers me stunned.

Fortunately, it shows up I don't have to state anything, Emily's foreheads scrunch over her eyes as she does a twofold take and broaden when she understands who it is perched on the bed before her "Kaitlyn? Kaitlyn Suarez?"

"That is me" I state, my voice sound piercing and unpredictable "how are you Emily?" I ask, sounding marginally more quiet.

Emily pulls a seat and sits close to the bed, motioning to my arm she takes a gander at it "I'm showing improvement over you it appears, as yet wrecking individuals at each given chance?" She prods prior to standing up "pardon me a second, I need to get a few supplies" and disregards rapidly leaving me again.

I take a progression of quieting breaths, my heart thumping unpredictably, I can't accept this is going on. I haven't seen or gotten with this lady in five years and afterward she simply appears suddenly and still has this significant impact on me. I need to get up and leave this spot, I'm enticed to go to the closest Target and purchase a needle and string to close the cursed thing up myself to make sure I don't need to see her. Yet, contrary to what own might think is best, I stay frozen in place and wind up anticipating her return.

At the point when she ventures back in through the window ornament I'm more arranged and really end up grinning at her.

She's equipped with provisions and expertly starts to wipe out my arm "this is an awful cut, how could you oversee it?" She asks discreetly.

I shake my head and murmur "screwing courier bicycle wrecked me" Emily stops briefly and looks into me with a quirked temple, I feign exacerbation at her and press together my lips "I'm very much aware of the incongruity. Presently would you say you will fix me Doctor Forester, or simply sit and make fun of me?"

Emily laughs and continues to work "you look great Kait, how's life been treating you?"

"Great, graduated top of my group, got an extraordinary temporary position and a decent friend network. You? I didn't understand you'd return to New York"

Emily at any rate has the goodness to look somewhat humiliated by my comment of her nonappearance from my life after she in a real sense vanished "about that..."

"Don't. It's fine. Genuinely however how are things for you? What's more, Charlotte? She became showbiz royalty yet?" Emily gazes toward me, an unusual little grin all the rage prior to moving her consideration back to the job that needs to be done.

"I'm fine, working insane hours here battling for a medical procedure time. Harvard was extraordinary! Didn't exactly complete top, however in the main five percent of my group which was sufficient to give me my decision of residency programs. Charlotte returned to London in the wake of being offered a lead in a phase play. We're... we're not together any longer. Haven't been for around nine months, she's really drawn in to a chap who went to class with my sibling."

Emily's not with Charlotte any longer? The news makes my sporadic heart beat considerably quicker and I quietly thank the sky that I'm in a clinic right now since I'm certain it's going to stop any second "I'm sorry to learn that" I mumble, Emily's eyes meet mine again and she takes a gander at me eagerly. I feel that attractive maneuver bringing me into her, still there and as solid as it generally seemed to be.

"Are you?" She asks unobtrusively. I gesture gradually, and we simply sit and gaze at one another for a since quite a while ago, drawn out second "all done." She checks the time and back at me "you were my last patient, if it's not all that a lot of an interruption how might you want to snatch a beverage with me? Make up for lost time?"

I don't figure I could grin any more extensive than I did at that time "I'd like that a ton. Where would it be advisable for me to hang tight for you?"

She restores my grin with a blindingly excellent one of her own and stands up, taking my diagram from the finish of the bed and marking it off "there's an entryway down the corridor. I need to get changed and afterward we can go to this extraordinary little bar. It's several traffic lights away" the words spout out of her however it's charming to tune in to. I'm simply happy that I'm at long last seeing her once more, that I'm at long last ready to invest energy with her again and hear her out chuckle.

I stand by anxiously in the anteroom, checking my watch like clockwork as I envision her return. I'm not distraught that she didn't stay in contact, it hurt like hellfire however where it counts I know why she did it. She was in an incomprehensible position yet it's diverse now, I can feel it. Quit losing track of the main issue at hand she may have another sweetheart.

I don't get an opportunity to berate myself for being over hopeful considerably more in light of the fact that Emily strolls towards me and she's changed out of her pale dim cleans and is glancing lovely in Levis and a thick weave dim sweater. Her grin makes my internal parts soften and nothing remains at this point but to stand and smile foolishly at her "you all set?" She inquires.

"Sure am." The stroll to the bar is decent, the city air is cool and lovely. We trade merriments as we go, filling in the holes freely for the past five years. The bar is little and comfortable, a long bar fills the back divider, uncovered block and different games memorabilia beautify the encompassing dividers. High tables and seats are specked around the focal point of the floor, stalls lounge around the edge. It's packed with individuals, talking among themselves and making the most of their night.

"What do you need?" She asks as we each sit on a stool toward the finish of the bar, Emily's hand waves noticeable all around flagging the barkeep.

"Simply a brews fine please." Placing our requests Emily goes to me and takes a gander at me eagerly, she takes a long beverage from the jug that is set before her and rests her free hand on top of mine.

"I will be immediate Kaitlyn, I'm too occupied to even consider bullshiting things any longer." I simply gesture, savoring her touch after so long "five years prior I settled on a decision, a decision I knew at that point and I'm considerably more certain presently was some unacceptable decision. I don't think a days passed by where I haven't considered you."

As much as her words fill me with satisfaction, I end up glaring a smidgen "I've held up quite a while to hear you state that, and I think you realize that. Yet, for what reason did you just cut me off the manner in which you did? For what reason didn't you attempt and connect previously? Like nine months prior when you and Charlotte separated?"

Emily moans and runs her hand through her hair "I needed to, I truly did. However, after the way I left things I was terrified that if I somehow managed to connect, suddenly after so long you'd berate me to piss and you'd reserve each privilege to, yet I have an inclination now that you're as glad to consider me to be I am to see you?" Her eyes search mine, searching for answers and I can just gesture.

I take a beverage of my lager and ribbon my fingers through hers "you have no clue. I missed you, in view of my affections for you as well as in light of the fact that you were my companion as well. So there's no sweetheart around now?"

Emily shakes her head and grins "no, I'm a free specialist. You?"

I smile "I can't recollect the keep going date I went on quit worrying about the last relationship I had." Emily's grin broadens before she downs her brew and turns around to me, her hands cup my face and she takes a gander at me eagerly.

"I need to kiss you" she says gruffly, turning my inner parts to goo, my breath leaves my body in a long murmur as I incline toward her hands.

"At that point kiss me" I murmur, my covers fall shut and my lips part somewhat, I feel Emily's warm breath all over as our lips are scarcely a hairs broadness separated. This is it, this is the thing that I've been hanging tight for every one of these years. I've needed this since the second I initially met her and it's going to occur. A progression of blaring coming from around the bar breaks the second and Emily pulls away, taking a gander at me contritely prior to pulling her pager from out of her pocket. Her foreheads wrinkle and she checks out the room, my eyes follow her look and many signals sounds out around the room, people all peer down at their pagers and afterward back up looking for a TV screen.

"Mike, hello Mike!" Emily calls the barman in a harsh voice "turn the news on" a progression of chorused demands from around the bar concurs and he hesitantly conforms to the solicitation of his supporters.

I contact Emily's arm, focusing on her me "is everything alright?" She pales and looks from me and back to the television screen, I follow her eyes and heave at the scene unfurling before me.

"We've gotten reports that a progression of impacts have occurred on different tram lines, many are suspected to have been injured and executed. We are as yet anticipating affirmation on whether this is a fear monger assault. Police have exhorted all suburbanites maintain a strategic distance from the tram where conceivable and take elective courses around the city..."

Emily takes a gander at me, a tormented appearance painted across her face, development around the bar wakes her up and she starts tying her hair back out of her face and hauls her wallet out and tosses a few bills down on the counter. "I need to go..."

I connect and cup her face, brushing my thumb across her cheek "I know" I state, her hand comes to up and covers mine holding my hand set up prior to transforming her lips into my palm and putting a kiss there. She moves rapidly and fishes a bunch of keys and a pen out of her pocket.

"This is my location, these are my condo keys. I truly need to complete this discussion however I don't have the foggiest idea what amount of time this will require. Go to my condo, make yourself at home." I simply gesture and she gives me a waiting look and plunges her head, squeezing her lips against my cheek making shudders run all over my back. I watch her advance out of the bar at speed and let out a long murmur, she's been gone not exactly a moment and I as of now miss her.

The stroll to her loft hushes up, I'm wracked with nerves at the prospect of going into her own space without her. But at the same time I'm discreetly satisfied that after so long separated she confides in me enough not to burglarize her. I laugh to myself at that idea and rapidly end up before a brownstone building. Twofold checking the location on the napkin, I stroll up the stoop gradually and pull out her keys. It takes a few attempts to pick the correct one yet I at last figure out how to get the entryway open and stroll up the steps to her loft. Giving myself access I close the entryway and glance around, the entire spot smells much the same as her and I feel myself unwind immediately.

The condo is so similar to Emily, clinically spotless and everything in its place. In the parlor outlined photographs decorate the generally clear dividers and I glance through them, photograph of Emily with a youngster I can just accept that is her sibling Max because of the striking likenesses between the two. Photos of her and her sibling with their folks independently, her mom looks harsh and cold. Her hardened stances and the manner in which her grin doesn't contact her virus eyes, the direct inverse to her dad. Emily looks a ton like her dad, the eyes, the hair tone, their grin. He's grinning in each photograph with his little girl, looking glad at her Harvard graduation as she remains there with his arm around her midsection in her cap and outfit. I grin at them all, getting an investigate her life I've never had the option to have.

I keep on investigating the loft room by room, when I arrive at the room I drift in the entryway prior to shutting the entryway again and moving back to the parlor. I feel fretful as I sit on the sofa and start flicking through different television slots, getting looks at the news and turning the station over when the tension kicks in that regularly does when anything awful occurs.

I resolve to get settled subsequent to being there for an hour and with no indication of Emily, so I dismiss my shoes from twist up toward the side of the love seat and pull the cover over me that is collapsed flawlessly on the back.

Somewhere close to a live update on the tram blasts and a discussion between purported specialists I snoozed off, in light of the fact that I'm woken by the sound of the loft signal sounding. I move as fast as my legs will convey me across the room and press the radio catch "hi?"

"Kaitlyn, it's Emily I need you to buzz me in. You have my keys" she sounds depleted is my first idea as I press the entryway discharge catch and speed tensely around the lobby sitting tight for her to show up.

The entryway opens and she closes it behind her gradually, her eyes discover mine and it's there once more. That pull, the snap noticeable all around between us, just this time there's nothing halting us both yielding to it. Neither of us speak, Emily tosses her rucksack onto the floor alongside the entryway and in three long walks shuts the distance between us. Taking my face in her grasp she pulls my lips to hers and kisses me immovably.

I consider flashes to be my eyelids as our mouths move together, my hands lay on her hips and I hold her to me immovably. Trim my body to the shapes of hers until we're only one individual. This is everything a first kiss ought to be, delicate however enthusiastic, wild yet saved, our lips fit together and move as one out of a way that feels right. Like they'd been doing it forever and were knowledgeable in the craft of kissing the other.

At the point when Emily pulls back she leans her temple against mine and kisses the tip of my nose "I've hung tight quite a while for that" she mumbles, I can hear my heart beating in my ears, there's nothing left but to lean my head against her chest and hold her near me. "I need to remain like this Kait, yet I need to shower and I need to eat" I pull my head back and gaze toward the lady before me and grin delicately, bringing my hand up I follow her lips and contact kiss her again delicately.

"Well go for a shower and I'll arrange you some food, what do you need?" Emily smiles down at me and shrugs her shoulders prior to venturing out of my grasp.

"Whatever you extravagant, there's certain menus in the cabinet close to the sink. Take your pick. I won't be long." I hang tight for her to enter the washroom and close the entryway, when I hear the water start to run I do a little turn and screech discreetly in merriment. I've recently kissed Emily, she's simply kissed me.

In a surprise I request some Chinese food and pay the conveyance fellow when he shows up and fire plating it up as Emily strolls back out the restroom drying her hair. My mouth goes dry at seeing her in some ball shorts and what resembles a soccer shirt as she cushions into the kitchen shoeless. She smiles when she sees me remaining at the counter and drops her towel into a hamper by her clothes washer prior to shutting the distance and strolling up behind me and folding her arms over my abdomen.

I promptly liquefy into her grasp and grin so wide I feel like my face will part in two, her breath on my ear makes me shudder somewhat and stop what I'm doing "I figure I could become acclimated to having you in my kitchen" she mumbles into my ear prior to kissing it daintily.

I snicker boisterously and put down the now vacant container as an afterthought prior to turning in her grasp, quirking an eyebrow at her I fold my arms over her shoulders and meet her eyes "five years of radio quiet and one kiss doesn't improve it, you have a great deal of making up to do."

She fakes hurt and brings a hand up to her chest "ooh, cheap shot. In any case, I'm capable" she runs her nose along the length of mine and kisses the tip daintily.

In the event that I was that sort of individual I'd presumably faint at that confirmation however I'm not all that I decide to attempt to chill out "you would be wise to be, I'd prefer not to be disillusioned." I drive her away daintily and get a plate from the counter "eat, sit and how about we talk" I point her toward her front room and push her tenderly on the back to make her move "do you have anything to drink?" I ask before she leaves the kitchen totally.

"Better believe it, ought to be a few lagers in the cooler" she brings out behind her, going to the fridge I discover four jugs and very little else. I shake my head prior to snatching two and getting my own plate from the counter and joining her in the parlor.

I give her a brew and she unscrews the top and takes a significant piece from it "I need this, much obliged." I take cues from her and sit with my legs tucked under me at the opposite finish of the lounge chair.

"I'm not amazed; there's nothing in your refrigerator separated from brew. When do you eat?"

She bites the food in her mouth and swallows prior to taking a gander at me, I notice how tired her eyes look before she talks "at the clinic ordinarily or I request in. I work ninety hour weeks, I'd work more in the event that they'd let me. Yet, they have a greatest hour limit for inhabitants" she takes another significant piece of food prior to forging ahead "would you approve of that? That is to say, I'm going off of the supposition that you'd need a relationship with me. I mean I trust that is the thing that you need. What do you need?"

I can't help the laugh that rises as I watch her mishandle with her words "Emily, I've needed you for quite a while. I never suspected I'd see you again never mind stay here in your condo, examining the conceivable outcomes of having a relationship with you." Suddenly my craving vanishes and I begin pushing the food around on my plate "I need to ask Em, for what reason did you quit conversing with me?"

Emily turns away from me and gazes blankly at the TV briefly, her eyebrows wrinkle over her eyes. I would prefer not to see her like this, yet I need to know why she just cut me off without even a word "Charlotte saw us moving together, perceived how close we were. She carried it up with me after we moved in together and gave me a final proposal, either focus on her and our relationship. Which implied cutting you off, or she'd return to London. I settled on some unacceptable decision, once more." Emily glances back at me with a particularly furious look, I feel my skin consume under it. She shakes her head and turns away once more "I am so sorry Kait, I would prefer not to burn through additional time with some unacceptable individual. So when she left and buggered off back to England, I needed to connect I truly did. Yet, I didn't have the foggiest idea how it would go down. In any case, I'm happy it was me that sewed you up today" she goes to smile at me and I return it, her hand connects and she pushes a lock of my hair behind my ear, her fingers following gradually down my neck. "I'm happy I get another opportunity at this."

"I actually can't accept this is occurring, I really liked you" that makes her chuckle and I can't resist the urge to participate. Emily puts her vacant plate down and gives me a look so brimming with want that I'm worried I will liquefy into a puddle on her lounge chair.

"Just HAD a pound? Past tense? Kaitlyn Suarez, you wound me..." she moves near me on the love seat, taking the plate from my hands and putting it on the table close to it. Her face is so near mine, her breath warm on my sharpened skin making it shiver with expectation.

"Almost certain I actually really like you, however I figure I should kiss you once more. You know, just no doubt?" I make an honest effort to fake impassion however I can feel my face heat, by and by my heart is beating so boisterously I'm shocked the neighbors can't hear it.

"I imagine that is a decent method to set up that..." she mumbles prior to pushing her lips against mine, one of her arms wrap around my shoulder, her different pulls me at my midriff holding me close. I can pretty much figure out how to tangle my fingers into her actually moist hair and pull her face hard against mine. At the point when I feel Emily run her tongue along my base lip, I shudder in her grasp and open my mouth readily to her. Her tongue contacts mine making me groan into the kiss, that one sound purposes an adjustment in the manner she kisses me. Her lips become additionally requesting against mine, her grasp on me fixes and I feel her push me back against the love seat. My heads swimming as it loads up with the vibe of her encompassing me, her weight on top of me, the manner in which she moves her lips from mine to kiss along my stunning and up to my ear.

At the point when I feel her pull at the flap with her teeth my eyes snap open, levelheadedness wins out and I have my first intellectual idea "Emily, Em... Stop" she pulls up unexpectedly and takes a gander at me, her chest hurls as she slows down to rest. I sit up and grin at her timidly "I think we need to back off" I clarify, measuring her cheek with my hand "I need to, good lord I truly need to yet we'd be going about it wrong on the off chance that we were to simply bounce into bed together at this moment and I don't need that and I realize you don't possibly" she doesn't utter a word, she simply folds her arm over my shoulder and pulls me to her. Inclining my head against her chest, I can hear her heart pulsating quick underneath my ear and it makes me grin to think I have that impact on her.

I feel her lips press against my hair and she murmurs "you're right, obviously you are. Other than if I'm being straightforward I'd likely nod off partially through and I envision you wouldn't be satisfied." I chuckle against her chest and shake my head.

"I can leave in case you're drained. How long did you work?"

"I'd recently reached the finish of a 36 hour stretch when I previously saw you, and afterward I was there for an additional five hours tonight and it was damnation. I don't need you to leave Kaitlyn, I've recently got you back." I notice the adjustment in her voice and sit up and move away from her. She takes a gander at me in disarray however I stand and intertwine her hand with mine and lead her to the room.

"Try not to misunderstand the thought Doctor Forester, yet you need to rest" I pull my sweater over my head and commencement my pants so I'm remaining there in my shirt and undies. Hands on my hips I attempt and look harsh when I see Emily's mouth fall open and her eyes meander the length of my body. "Close your mouth you're getting flies, they're simply legs. You don't need me to leave, genuinely I would prefer not to go, so we will get into bed and you can reveal to me how it was for you this evening or we can simply rest. In any case, you will rest" I point at her and movement for her to get into bed with my finger before I pull the covers down and move in.

It pauses for a minute for her turn, yet she does, I hold my arm out for her and she takes a gander at it prior to taking the greeting and cuddling right up front "I can't recollect the last time somebody really held me. It's normally the reverse way around" she murmurs as I pull her tight to me and kiss her hair, running my nose through it and breathing in her still recognizable smell.

"Not even Charlotte?" She solidifies in my arms and I can't resist the urge to feign exacerbation "Emily you were with her for quite a while, I'm not going to evade your previous as it didn't make a difference." She gazes toward me through the dimness and I can see the faintest grin play all the rage.

"You're very adult aren't you?" I can't resist the urge to chuckle at her perception however I shrug my shoulders and kiss her sanctuary.

"I shock myself now and again. How terrible was it this evening? I saw bits on the news however I nodded off."

Emily shivers and goes calm briefly, I let my fingers follow little circles over her back. As yet delighting at the way that I'm laid in bed with the lady I've been pining after since dinosaurs wandered the earth "it was awful. I've seen a great deal over the most recent two years, multivehicle crashes, thefts turned out badly, stabbings, attacks, the strangest mishaps. However, this evening was something different, it was disarray. I'm preparing to be a specialist so I have a lovely strong stomach however a portion of the things I saw..." I feel her shiver again and tip her face up to take a gander at me with the fingers I twist under her jaw.

Brushing my lips against hers delicately I lean my head against hers and murmur "you can stop on the off chance that you want..."

"I would prefer not to, really it's ideal to have the option to converse with somebody about it. It was the families that exacerbated it, they overflowed the medical clinic requesting to know where their friends and family were. Regardless of whether they were alive or dead, as a second year occupant we're given a gathering of understudies to coach so I set one of mine with the assignment of keeping them refreshed so I could scour in on one of the injury medical procedures. I discovered them crying in the women latrines when I got out in light of the fact that she needed to tell a man that his better half and two children hadn't made it. She discovered their bodies in the funeral home, she had an extraordinary thought to photo everybody that came in with one of those polaroid cameras and set up two notification sheets, one for survivors one for the perished and had the family compose their names and data on them." She stops briefly and I hold her more tight to me "at any rate, this one person wouldn't quit bothering her so she requested portrayals and that is the means by which she discovered them. I felt for her, it's one of the principal things you figure out how to do as specialists. Quite possibly the most significant too, that doesn't make it any simpler."

"Also, you do this energetically on the grounds that?" I joke, feeling her giggle against me.

"Since when it goes right, it feels astonishing. I put in half a month chipping away at the paed's floor a few months back and there was this child, joe he was called. Eight years of age, he was brought into the world with an uncommon type of malignancy and had experienced 77 unique medical procedures since he was conceived, alongside radiation therapy and chemotherapy. At any rate long story short, he'd been on the giver list for another kidney for around eight months, all being great and we found a match that would be it. His specialist had figured out how to corner that jerk to his last kidney and sincerely it was sticky for some time. Yet, when we got that call and he emerged from a medical procedure effectively, I saw the delight on his mom's face and that made all the crap you experience day in day out justified, despite all the trouble. They kid has a shot to live for an additional eighty years and I had an influence in that."

The manner in which she talks so energetically about it is so charming to tune in to, I feel my heart swell as I hear her out go on about it "you know, I don't think I've ever heard you talk about something like this. You generally used to be so solid and formal, well more often than not."

Emily laughs against my chest "definitely, in the event that I recollect properly you used to ask me where the stick had gone?" I snicker at that memory and feign exacerbation through the murkiness.

"You recollect effectively, in the most bizarre way I really missed battling with you a smidgen."

"Me as well, consistently got me hot when you'd advise me to go screw myself. I like them feisty" I crush her more tight, attempting my hardest to overlook the consuming sensation of want in the pit of my stomach. She comes to up and pecks my lips rapidly prior to laughing gently "don't stress I'm not going to bounce you."

"I'm not stressing, I'm more stressed that I don't think I'd stop you on the off chance that you did, and I implied what I said before." I murmur, feeling all my sincere goals evaporate in a moment when I picture the lady in my arms stripped and squirming under my ministrations.

Emily pulls me down for a moderate, waiting kiss prior to moving endlessly from me, pulling me with her so I'm spooning her from behind "I realize you coddled, I'm happy you said it." She connects her fingers between the ones on my correct hand and carries them to her lips "around evening time I'm glad to rest this way" she yawns noisily and I nestle in not far behind her.

"Rest Em" I mumble into her neck, feeling rest crawling up on me. I need to remain wakeful and appreciate each experience with the lady in my arms. Her warm body against my front, the manner in which she fits impeccably against the shapes of my body like we were made to resemble this together. In any case, as her breathing levels out, rest hauls me down and I capitulate to it rapidly.

***

At the point when I wake toward the beginning of the day neither one of us has moved, I actually have my arms at her mercy around her, her fingers are as yet bound through mine and it makes me grin. I hazard a look at my wrist watch and

83

moan deep down, despite the fact that it's still early, in case I will make it to chip away at time and still have the option to return home to shower and change. I need to leave now.

Gradually and cautiously I attempt to unravel myself from Emily without waking her, I do not understand if she's working today however she needs to rest. I'm sure I've pulled off it as I move out of the bed and start pulling my pants on discreetly. When I hear her speak, I leap out of my skin "sneaking off without bidding farewell Kait? Pleasant." I stop and watch her turn over and prop her head facing the pad.

I grin timidly as I attach my pants and lift my sweater up off of the floor "I need to go to work and I need to return home and change. I would not like to wake you." I pull my sweater on and creep back up the bed to Emily where I kiss her immovably. When I pull back I realize I'm smiling like a crackpot when she mirrors my grin back at me "what about supper around evening time? My treat." I ask as I run my nose along the length of hers, she clamps down on her lip and shakes her head.

"I wouldn't i be able to was intended to be working from early afternoon, however I've been given the morning off by my joining in yet it implies I must force the super late shift this evening." I can't battle the appearance of dissatisfaction all over, yet that is brief when I have an alternate thought.

84

"What time do you generally wrap up?"

"Presumably around six am the reason?"

"Since... you should go to mine after you finish and I'll make you breakfast. Or then again supper or whatever you call the feast you have after you finish a night move." I kiss her cheek and the tip of her nose and watch the grin that breaks out across her highlights.

"That might be the best offer I've had in some time"

"Great, I'll record my cell and my location and leave it in the kitchen. You should return to rest." I kiss her one final time before hesitantly pulling ceaselessly and holding up. Obstinate as usual, Emily tosses the covers back and strolls me to the entryway, I can't conceal how happy I am however when she kisses me one final time before I leave with the guarantee that she'll call me before she begins her work day and let me know whether she needs to remain at the emergency clinic late.

I leave hesitantly however nothing that happens today will destroy my positive mind-set and it seems like Lady Luck is my ally. The primary taxi I banner stops for me and gets me back to my condo in record time meaning I possess a lot of energy for a long shower and a fast difference in garments prior to taking off the entryway and strolling energetically to the theater.

Work is routine and when my mid-day break comes I have an inclination that I've checked my telephone multiple times. I need Emily to call, in the couple of hours I've been away from her I miss her voice. Be that as it may, I recall how it felt when she originally kissed me and that it was so great to get up earlier today wrapped up close to her and I wind up running my fingers across my lips and grinning like an affection wiped out young person.

"What are you so upbeat about?" Gregory, my chief, at last asks me. I'd saw him watching me with interest for the duration of the day yet he'd kept quiet up to this point.

I moan happily and grasp my hands to my chest "I ran into an old companion from school the previous evening and it was magnificent." His eyebrows raise into his hair line and he grins at me "what are you grinning at?"

"Does this companion have a name?"

I moan again and document the papers he hands to me "Emily, she graduated pre-prescription my first year yet we were... close.

She headed out to Harvard drug school and we kind of lost touch."

"In any case, presently you're back in touch and that has you overjoyed like a school young lady?"

"Essentially, better believe it." I answer "it's insane, we had this association in those days yet nothing could happen in light of the fact that she had a sweetheart. In any case, presently, no sweetheart and still this crazy association. I remained the evening and no in no way like that occurred." I call attention to before he asks "yet when she kissed me. Firecrackers Gregory. Real firecrackers."

He looks on at me in delight and chuckles "I don't think I've ever seen you this stricken previously. It's ideal to see, helps me to remember when I initially met Simon."

A little grin plays all the rage as he gets a distant look in his eyes, obviously reviewing some ancient history I don't know I need to think about. "you folks are amazing together" I scold as I slap him tenderly on the arm. Fortunately, that is the keep going I hear on the subject of my adoration life and the remainder of the evening flies by.

As I bungle with the keys to my loft, adjusting basic food item sacks in dubiously in my arms, my phone chooses to ring. Hurrying in and unloading the packs inelegantly on the counter I answer it rapidly, holding my breath in the expectation of hearing my #1 English pronunciation.

"Hi?"

I'm not frustrated "in this way, I needed to call before yet I got a call from my going to with the proposal to scour in on an amazing a medical procedure on the off chance that I arrived rapidly so I settled on my decision. Furthermore, I don't think twice about it." I can hear the grin in her voice and it makes me laugh.

I wedge the telephone between my ear and shoulder as I start unloading food supplies "I'm not even distraught, I can for all intents and purposes hear you grinning. Other than that how's your day been angel?" I disregard the way that I've quite recently called her darling and continue ahead with the job needing to be done.

"Fine, dozed a large portion of it. Not just as I did the previous evening but rather I was broken. Plans for around evening time?"

I moan and close the cooler entryway prior to inclining toward the kitchen counter "supper for one, observe some junky TV and head to bed early. Seeing as I've offered to prepare breakfast for some unpredictable Brit and some wicked hour in the first part of the day." I grin at the sound of her voice through the telephone and bite on my base lip.

"Well what about after this unpredictable Brit's had said breakfast she offers to take you out for the day seeing as she has her first three day weekend in a month tomorrow and can't think about a superior method to spend it?"

Butterflies fly through my stomach and my heart skirts a beat at her words "I'd love it, what do you have as a primary concern?"

"All things considered, notwithstanding the way that I've lived in New York on and off for a very long time or thereabouts, I've never been site seeing? So we should do all the messy traveler stuff? Realm State Building, Statue of Liberty, Times square? And afterward I'll take you out to supper. Like a legitimate date."

The idea makes me smile and my cheeks flush "that is awesome."

"Great, I must scramble infant. I'm being paged, I'll attempt call or text before you rest yet things get insane here around evening time now and again."

"Certainly, talk soon. I'll see you toward the beginning of the day." She detaches the call rapidly however I couldn't care less, I'm actually radiating at her calling me child and that I'll be seeing her tomorrow. We hobnobbed in school, however tomorrow will be unique, tomorrow I'll will kiss her.

Chapter six: You and I

At the point when my alert sounds at 5:30 I moan noisily and quietness it, keeping my tops solidly shut. Just when I understand what's going on today and recall why my alert is set for so promptly toward the beginning of the day do I straight up and climb across the bed for my phone. Checking it energetically I see I have two uninitiated messages from Emily and my stomach hitches, anticipating that she should drop her arrangements with me because of some crisis at the clinic. Fortunately those apprehensions are immediately exposed to rest when I them:

Sorry it's late, you're likely snoozing yet I guaranteed you a goodnight text. So goodnight, I trust you rest in a way that is better than I do on the grounds that I can't quit considering you, or your lips and how they felt against mine. See you toward the beginning of the day excellent. X

I'm completing somewhat right on time by some wonder so I'll be at yours in about thirty minutes. I trust you'll be up on the grounds that I'm hungry! See you soon x

Poop, the last one was sent at 5:10 along these lines, extraordinary, I have ten minutes to get up and attempt and look mostly adequate before she turns up. I fly around my room abruptly of garments and unadulterated frenzy as I dress in pants and a button up shirt, choosing ease over style I pull my hair up in a high pig tail. I've quite recently wrapped up making my bed when the loft signal sounds, I don't press the radio knowing precisely what it's identity is, I press the entryway delivery and stand by anxiously for her.

The butterflies are spinning out of control in my stomach when the entryway thumps and my face feels like it will part when I open it and see her there. She doesn't hold on to be welcomed in, she grins at me as she walks through the entryway and takes my face in her grasp and rapidly asserts my lips with her own. Some place during the kiss I hear the entryway shut before she starts strolling me back against the closest divider, catching me among it and her as she keeps on kissing me ravenously. I handle her by her hips and pull her flush against me, shutting any extra space between us as we kiss with enthusiasm.

At the point when she pulls separated we're both winded and gazing at one another eagerly "you made the guarantee of breakfast?" She jested, gasping marginally, her eyes consuming into mine splendidly.

I gesture, my dry mouth incapable to talk, breakfast right currently is the farthest thing from my psyche. At the present time all I need to do is drag her to the room and strip her gradually, kissing each inch of revealed skin. I shake my head, needing to scatter my grimy musings and spotlight on the motivation behind why she's in reality here. "I did, yet you'll have to release me first." Emily plunges her head and kisses me one final time prior to venturing back and liberating me. I feign exacerbation and grasp her hand, getting her through to the kitchen with me. I pull out one of the stools at the kitchen island and point at it "sit."
"You've gotten bossy, you realize that?" She jests as my backs stopped people in their tracks in the cooler. Pulling out all the elements for breakfast I set them on the counter and give her a harsh look.

"I've been called more terrible, right, so I did some googling and discovered what a mainstream alternative for breakfast is back in England and clearly there's this thing called a 'Full English?' I've figured out how to discover the majority of the things for it, so that is the thing that you're having. Any protests?" She radiates back at me with a quirked eyebrow and eyes the thing on the counter.

"You googled breakfast thoughts? That is delightful, yet additionally exceptionally insightful. Much obliged to you."

I smile at her, satisfied she's cheerful "do you need tea while I cook or with your morning meal?"

"A cup currently would be incredible. Would i be able to effectively help?"

I shake my head at her prior to going to fill the pot and setting it to bubble "simply stay there and look pretty. You're amusing to take a gander at?"

"View isn't excessively pitiful from this side either, particularly when you get things from the base cabinets." I take a gander at her from behind me and she winks at me, making my heart race. I feign exacerbation at her and make an honest effort to preparing breakfast without consuming anything.

93

***

"That was stunning! That eatery was so acceptable, where did you discover it?" I ask as we stroll once more into my condo subsequent to going through a mystical day together.

Emily follows me and hangs her jacket up over the rear of one of the kitchen stools as I pull out a jug of wine and open up it rapidly "by complete mishap. A coworker set me up on a terrible arranged meet up, she was totally exhausting however the unrivaled redeeming quality of the night was the food. I return time to time in transit home from work and they take care of it so I can take it home with me."

Pouring two glasses I push one towards her and we clear our path through to the parlor where we rapidly sit near one another. "Well it was extraordinary, truth be told the entire day has been superb. Best date I've ever been on" I take a taste of wine and lean my head-on her shoulder "despite the fact that, I imagine that had more to do with the organization than what we."

"You're an incredible sentimental aren't you Ms. Suarez?" I shrug and nestle her neck, kissing the skin just beneath her ear delicately and grinning to myself when I see her shudder somewhat.

"It's been known." I lean my head on her shoulder briefly prior to sitting up to take a taste of wine, we sit in a charged quietness together. The air encompassing us popping with expectation, turning my head marginally to take a gander at her I find her watching me eagerly. Her shining green eyes focused all the rage, I run my tongue along my base lip, suspicious that some wine has accumulated there. I see her chest rise and fall rapidly as she pauses to rest, when her eyes flick up to meet mine the consuming desire in them is irrefutable and it mixes something in me.

Silently we close the distance among us and our lips meet in the mildest grasp, pulling back we observe one another. The air between us turns out to be thick, making it practically hard to relax. Emily assumes responsibility, and I'm happy. Putting her wine glass on the table toward the finish of the couch prior to turning around to me and removing mine from my hand and putting it down with hers. She puts both of her hands on my shoulders and pushes me back against the couch and arranges herself between my legs, I'm powerless to stop her. My arms tangle themselves around her back, grasping onto her solid, conditioned shoulders for dear life.

We don't express a word to one another as we lie that way, Emily's glow encompasses me as her body pushes against mine. Fitting to each shape impeccably.

Bringing her lips down to mine she kisses me at a tortuously moderate rate, stirring up the fire that is presently consuming me. Her hands meander my body, running all over my sides over my shirt prior to making the excursion down my thighs towards my knees. As though by nature my legs fold themselves over her midriff, pulling her hips down to meet mine. At the point when she groan in my mouth, any smidgen of restraint I may have had left rapidly evaporates. My hands move from her shoulders to the top catch of her shirt and with bungling fingers start to loosen them individually. Her shirt detached, my hands move to her shoulders and I start to drive the material away from her shoulders. Emily lifts her mouth away from mine and takes a gander at me questioningly, stilling my hands "you're secure with this? The previous evening you said you needed to stand by." She asks energetically.

I pull her mouth down to mine and kiss her hard prior to pushing her off to polish pushing her shirt off and dropping it to the floor "I've altered my perspective" I state prior to sitting up to move my lips along her sternum and down the delicate skin between her bosoms, I hear her attract her breath through her teeth in a murmur making me grin against her skin.

Emily pulls my face up to hers and cases my mouth again in a short however angry kiss, her mouth moving from mine to run along my jaw and down the segment of my neck. Her lips on my skin sets it ablaze, as they move along my neck and shoulders leaving a consuming path afterward. I moan in dissatisfaction when Emily pulls her mouth away from my skin and takes a gander at me with a mindful articulation "we can stop in case you don't know, I mean I need this. I need you, yet not to the detriment of whatever this is..."

I can't resist the urge to feign exacerbation with her as I sit up marginally, driving her away a smidgen. My hands start at my top catch and busts open it "normally Em, the subject of English appeal you have going gets me hot. At the present time, it's super irritating" I loosen my catches gradually, my eyes not leaving her face "I need this, I need you more than I've ever needed anybody" my shirt falls open and I hear Emily get her breath in a sharp murmur as I push it open and disregard it. Dropping it to the floor with hers "presently you have a decision, we can stop and simply nestle once more. Or then again you can take me to bed like I realize you need."

I don't get opportunity to think or state any longer, on the grounds that in the following breath I'm being gathered up in Emily's arms, my legs wrapped immovably around her midsection, her hands holding my rear end firmly. She squashes her lips against mine hard and starts helping me through the loft, I'm completely confounded when she quits moving and breaks the kiss "I don't have the foggiest idea where your room is" she concedes timidly.

"Down the hallway, first on the left" I don't sit tight for her to move or speak, I guarantee her mouth with my own and kiss her covetously. Nipping at her base lip with my teeth prior to smoothing the delicate skin with my tongue, with one hand I reach behind me to unsnap the fasten of my bra and remove it from me rapidly, tossing it behind me. I feel Emily groan into my mouth as she opens the room entryway and in the wake of making a couple of more strides, stores me down on it prior to creeping up and moving back between my legs.

Her head plunges down and her tongue follows the length of my neck, my shoulders and my chest before her mouth encompasses one of my bosoms, her tongue flicking against the generally close areola. "Ok," I murmur as my head inclines back and my body curves against the bed, pushing me against her. I pull her mouth back to mine, my hands haul down her back to her bra catch where I bumble with it until it comes fixed, she lifts herself away sufficiently long to pull it off before her skin meets mine. The sensation of her warmed skin pushing against mine resembles a disclosure making me heave against her lips. The manner in which my skin shivers at the contact resembles nothing I've ever felt previously, and the moan that gets away from her lips reveals to me she feels it as well.

Emily's hands run down the length of my sides, following the bend of my abdomen and hips until she arrives at the highest point of my pants. Burning through no time, she pops the catch and bows up to more readily test the denim down my sanity prior to storing them on the floor. Her eyes enlarge and her teeth close over her base lip as she drinks in seeing me in my undies, the way she's taking a gander at me right currently causes me to feel provocative and needed. Nobody's consistently seen me like this previously and I have never been so sure of anything in my life when I feel that I don't need anybody to take a gander at me the manner in which she is currently, other than the lady floating above me.

At the point when she moves herself back over me she has an odd grin all over, my shaking fingers follow her facial structure and she inclines toward my touch, her eyes shutting. "I've contemplated this significantly throughout the long term" she mumbles "of at last being with you the manner in which I ought to have been, it wasn't right" she gets my hand in hers and places delicate kisses to every one of my fingertips lastly my palm "I realize it wasn't right, however I was unable to stop myself. You overwhelmed me, you actually do."

Her words, her touch, the manner in which she's causing me to feel just adds to the fire consuming inside me. Her hands following the forms of my stomach prior to stopping at the highest point of my clothing, her lips follow the way her hands have quite recently taken, leaving my skin shivering afterward. Her nose runs along the length of my silk covered focus before she puts a delicate kiss simply over my clit making me pant and handle at the bed blankets. "You smell divine" I hear her mumble against my sex not long before her long fingers guide into the highest point of my clothing and gradually strips it away from me, uncovering me to her.

In one smooth motion she takes me in her mouth and flicks her tongue against my swollen stub, making my hips jettison up of the bed. Emily's hands grasp my hips as she attempts to keep me still while she has intercourse to me with her mouth. Her tongue whirls and tests, switching back and forth between its delicate level skimming over my cozy overlays and skewering my passage.

My body starts to move ever more elevated until it's wavering on a slope, taking steps to tumble over the edge at any second. I don't need it to end, I need to live at this time everlastingly as my toes twist and my head whips from side to side. Feeling Emily groan against me is the thing that sends me over the edge, I get down on her name as I come unraveled against her lips and hold the bedsheets so firmly I'm sure my knuckles have turned white. She laps away delicately briefly prior to slithering back up my body, kissing my stomach, bosoms and chest as she goes until she kisses me profoundly. Sliding her tongue into my mouth exotically, I can taste my climax all the rage and it makes me shiver. Moving off of me she pulls me tight against her chest as I assemble my breath, my brains reeling at what's simply occurred. Every one of those months in school my first year where I fantasized about this, poop even after that when she vanished off the substance of the earth, I actually considered this with her. Also, it's more than I actually might have needed it to be.

"Curious what you might be thinking?" She mumbles, her hands following examples over my exposed skin. I prop myself up on my elbow and respect her nicely until my eyes leave her ideal face and takes in the remainder of her. Bare from the midsection up, she's a treat to take a gander at. Strong abs, spunky and amazing bosoms, conditioned arms and the hottest hips I think I've ever seen.

"Indeed, I'm valuing this right now" I state as I trail a finger over her stomach and clamp down on the edge of my lip when she recoils, making her muscles tense and my crotch to jerk accordingly. "You have a mind boggling body, I do have one protest however."

"Furthermore, what is that?" She asks, a trace of delight in her voice.

I see her face and raise an eyebrow prior to measuring her sex with my hand over the material of her pants, she wheezes and glances back at me through hooded eyes "you're wearing to an extreme degree to an extreme" I answer, my fingers strolling their way down her firm stomach to her pants where I unfasten her belt and pop the catches rapidly. She needs no further support to strip herself and soon she's as bare as me with a poop eating smile put across her face.

As I slide down her body, pushing her so she's on her back, I roost myself between her legs and let my lips trail up within her thighs. The presumptuous smile that was all over starts to slip as her eyes stay fixed on mine as she watches me kiss every one of her thighs gradually. Feeling the muscles there dance underneath my lips, when I arrive at the criminal of her legs where they meet her crotch, my teeth close around the delicate skin there and she groans out loud. That groan is effectively the hottest thing I've ever heard and that is all the consolation I require to take her in my mouth energetically.

***

I lay spread across her bare chest, the sound of her heart pulsating moderate and even underneath my ear spreads a warm satisfaction through me and I grin against her skin. Emily's fingers are playing with my hair, her other arm twisted around my shoulders holding me near her. "I'd much the same as to call attention to, I never head to sleep with somebody on the principal date" I state contemplatively against her chest.

I feel the vibrations of her chuckle through her chest and prop my head up on the arm I have hung across her, her eyes meet mine and they hold a glow as she takes a gander at me. "You'll be satisfied to realize that neither do I, truth be told up till now I've just ever been with one other individual" this stuns me a tad and I eccentricity an eyebrow.

"Truly? Be that as it may, unquestionably you've dated a smidgen over the most recent nine months?"

She shrugs her shoulders and kisses the tip of my nose "I have, however I ended up contrasting them all with you and them failing to measure up so nobody truly made it past the subsequent date."

This affirmation makes my heart vacillate as I laugh innocently "it's so peculiar, I've been doing likewise since I initially met you. Indeed, even at school I'd date yet I'd end up contrasting everybody with you and surrendering when they didn't coordinate." She grins at me adoringly, my finger starts drawing circles on the delicate skin between her bosoms "what time are you grinding away tomorrow?" I ask discreetly, not needing her to leave me.

"five am. In any case, it implies I can leave at a good time and take you out to supper on the off chance that you don't have plans?"

"I don't have plans, you can remain here again in the event that you like. I need to work throughout the day Saturday, we have three exhibitions that day and Gregory demands I'm there to help the entire day" I feign exacerbation and murmur at the substantialness in my chest at the prospect of parting ways from her.

Emily kisses my brow and looks insightful briefly "this might be pompous however I need to be with you and I need this to work. I like that we both have occupied work routines however I'd be glad to spend the same number of evenings as I can like this." She presses me to her firmly, and in spite of nearly detesting myself for it, I faint at her words.

In a snapshot of unconstrained idea, I give her a fast peck on the lips and bounce up off of the bed and cushion out of the room stripped. Taking the extra keys to the condo out of the cabinet in the lobby, I return into my room and bow on the bed with her. "State no on the off chance that you need, however you should have these" I state prior to pushing the keys into her hand "is anything but a proposition to be engaged and I'm not requesting that you move in, yet evenings when you're remaining here and working late or beginning early or whatever you can go back and forth however you see fit." hold my breath while I sit tight for her reaction, my eyes stuck to her face as I check her response. Her eyes are wide and her jaws slack as she looks from me to the key and back once more. "Crap" I state, feeling the cut of disillusionment and the sting of dismissal as she keeps on staying there quiet "simply fail to remember it. Sorry. I wasn't think... mmph" she cuts me off by squeezing her lips to mine.

At the point when she pulls back her eyes are brilliant and her face has a heart halting grin extended across it "shut up, I love it. Much obliged, I er I don't have an extra key" she concedes as she rubs the rear of her neck "however I'll get one cut tomorrow after work."

"Along these lines, does this mean we're, I don't have a clue... a couple?" I stammer out, feeling my face go redder with each word.

Emily snickers and grasps her chest and faints drastically "gracious Kaitlyn, you're smooth route with words makes my heart ripple. A particularly powerful suggestion one thinks that its difficult to can't." I push her energetically and fold my arms against my chest, my base lip extends out in a sulk and this showcase of resentment simply makes her giggle stronger. Her arms fold over my neck and she pulls me back down to the bed with her "you're such a washout, yet I'd be glad to consider you my failure. No doubt, we're a couple infant. It's lovable you needed to inquire." She kisses my head, my cheeks, my nose and my lips prior to drawing the covers over-top us.

Her arms wrap defensively around me and I cuddle against her chest and moan "you're a genuine annoyance" I mumble lethargically.

"What's more, you're a freaking sentimental, presently rest. A few of us need to work in the first part of the day" I place my fingers over her lips to quiet her, my eyelids feeling hefty, she snickers delicately against them prior to kissing the tips tenderly.

Chapter seven: London Calling

Emily and I had been dating for around a month and a half when she asks me something I truly wasn't anticipating. Sitting at the middle island in my kitchen, having breakfast on one of the uncommon mornings we have off together I realize somethings ticking in that lovely top of hers as she pushes her eggs around her plate. I was sleeping when she returned home from work the previous evening and she's hushed up throughout the morning. I watch her cautiously over the edge of my espresso mug as I assume a taste and position it down gradually "Emily?" I ask, getting her to murmur her affirmation, her eyes not leaving her plate. "Is an off-base thing?"

She shakes her head and puts her fork down, her eyes actually stuck on her plate as she speaks "I need to ask you something" she states unassumingly, making my stomach fix tensely.

"Indeed, continue ahead with it at that point" I react, my fingers drumming an anxious cadence on the ledge. Her eyes eat up and she connects and puts her hand over mine, stilling them.

"I have some yearly leave coming up in half a month, I'm going to London for about fourteen days for my sibling's wedding. I need you to accompany me."

"That is an assertion, not an inquiry." I comment, the uneasiness that was in playing ruin in my stomach currently supplanted with fervor.

I supress a giggle when she feigns exacerbation at me and fixes me with a hard gaze "will you accompany me? Please?" I don't answer immediately, appreciating seeing the normally formed and shy specialist wriggling apprehensively "I need you to meet my family and I need to show you my old neighborhood. Try not to stress over cash, I have airmiles I can use for your ticket and we can remain with my father. I typically do and he's as of now said he'd gladly have you as well..."

"Emily..." I contribute prior to remaining to move before her, I separate her legs and remain between them. My arms wrap around her shoulders and I kiss her jaw "I'd love to go with you, I'm owed some get-away. I'll need to clear it with Gregory yet I don't see there being any issues. Just content me with the dates so I can ask him later." I peck her on the lips and start clearing the dishes, while she stays there somewhat dumbstruck.
I fondle her drag behind me while I remain at the sink flushing the plates prior to placing them in the dishwasher. Her arms fold over my abdomen and she nips my ear cartilage with her teeth "you let me babble like a moron when from the beginning you realized you planned to state yes? You're an abhorrent lady

108

Kaitlyn Suarez." She husks in my ear making me shudder in her grasp.

"Nothing more needs to be said. I appreciate watching you wriggle" I counter, her sharp admission of breath makes me need to crush my thighs together. She has a particularly crazy impact on me, it resembles she has a design to my drive and realizes each sensitive and perplexing catch to push without putting forth any attempt.

Emily compels me to pivot and face her, her eyes are igniting with unbridled desire as she watches me cautiously. She doesn't utter a word, she simply takes one of my wrists and moves my hand underneath the abdomen band of her night robe until its squeezing against her hill. "You appreciate watching me wriggle?" She mumbles, her lips moving against mine as she talks. I gesture and push my fingers against her, feeling the proof of her excitement covering them as I discover her clit and flick against it hard making her groan "at that point make me wriggle" and with that she covers my mouth with hers and deliveries my wrists to do however i see fit her. My fingers move lower until I slide two within her and twist them up, hitting the fix of nerves that never neglects to make her come. One of my new most loved spend times is making Emily come, the manner in which she looks, the manner in which her entire body tenses is effectively the hottest thing I've ever seen. My thumb presses against her clit as I start working my way all through her, she inclines her hips up, driving me more profound. Her mouth delivers mine and she covers her face in my shoulder and shuts her teeth against the law breaker of my neck.

I feel her fix around me before her peak covers my hand, her breath is hot against my neck as she gasps intensely. I attempt to eliminate my fingers yet her grasp around my wrist fixes briefly before I hear her talk energetically "just, allow me a moment." I gesture, driving her hair away from her face and covering her delicate skin in kisses.

The manner in which she looks presently, flushed, winded and just screwed, with an odd little grin playing all the rage, she looks so awesome. "I love you," my eyes enlarge as the words sneak off of my tongue. I need to connect into the air and power them back into my mouth when Emily's head gobbles up and her eyes go as wide as mine.

"What?"

I swallow and run my tongue along my base lip "I said that I love you." I'm mindful that this isn't the most sentimental approach to tell your better half that you love her unexpectedly, after an extemporaneous fast in and out in the kitchen while your fingers are as yet covered within her, yet I understand following a moment of her simply gazing at me that I've amounted to nothing more in my life than I do those three words.

"I love you as well." She murmurs, her green eyes gaze at mine seem watery as we simply remain there taking a gander at one another. I grin bashfully, reflecting hers prior to shutting the distance and kissing her delicately.

***

"Are you prepared Kaitlyn?" Emily calls from outside the room entryway, we've been in London for two days as of now and it's been incredible. Her father has invited me like an old companion and I've adored each moment I've spent here up until now. Today, I will observe some soccer match with both of them and Emily's sibling, Maxie and I've been talented a shirt to wear.

I leave the room and raise an eyebrow at my better half as she for all intents and purposes disrobes me with her eyes "don't see me like that. I don't care for soccer but then here I am wearing this" I pick at the material in contempt "all set to my first soccer match, since I realize the amount it intends to you. What even is Arsenal?"

Emily chuckles at me and pulls me to her, her hands sitting on my hips "a couple of tips to get you during that time child. One," she kisses my nose and runs the length of it with hers "it would be ideal if you quit calling it 'soccer' it's football. Local people get a whiff of that soccer bollocks and they'll send a lynch horde for you. Two," she kisses the edge of my lips delicately and runs her lips along my jaw to my correct ear, successfully creeping me out "you look so screwing hot in that, I'm anticipating seeing you out of it and in particular three," her teeth close over my ear cartilage before she kisses her way to my other ear and kisses the base of it delicately "Armory are simply the best footie group on God's green earth and you'll do well to recollect that." I feel her slap my can energetically and I push her shoulder hard.

"You're such an ass once in a while." I rebuke her, slipping my arms around her shoulders, gnawing my lip when I feel her hands press my behind eagerly.

"I know, yet we both realize it gets you wet so I make no arrangements on halting it." She smiles at me and I can't resist the urge to feign exacerbation in fake scorn.

"Sheesh, how the fuck did I figure out how to go gaga for a particularly sentimental?" She kisses me hard on the lips and takes my hands in hers, kissing them both prior to driving me down the steps.

"I don't have the foggiest idea, yet you got pretty fortunate with me" she jokes and we stroll down the steps laughing together.

We venture into the kitchen connected at the hip, Mark, Emily's father, is finding a spot at the table with a paper concealing his face. "Both of you about all set?" He asks, his accents a lot more grounded than Emily's. I never acknowledged until we arrived how her time in the States has mollified her complement a few.

Emily stores me in a seat at the table and starts pouring us both espresso from the pot on the work surface "pretty much, I've done what I can to instruct the Yank and you have my full gift to leave her to her own gadgets on the off chance that she alludes to it as soccer once more" she says as she places a cup before me.

"Tsk, I am sorry yet it's hard to simply change what I know for the time being Em. Football to me is a totally unique game to what it is here, and in case I'm being straightforward I don't cherish that all things considered!"

Imprint simply laughs at me and winks at me over his paper "you've recently been watching some unacceptable sort. Truly, I simply go to the games for the air and the lager. Is anything but a tasteful issue however we love it don't we nut?"

I grin at Emily's redden at her old pet name and she sinks into her seat a bit "what time's Maxie arriving?" I raise an eyebrow at her smooth difference in subject and snicker into my espresso as I take a taste. Both of them trade some energetic talk until the sound of the entryway opening and shutting occupies them adequately long to stop.

Max, is tall, expansive and uproarious. Furthermore, I promptly love him. Emily shoots up out of her seat and gives herself wholeheartedly to her sibling who scoops her up into a major huge squeeze. At the point when she at long last segregates herself from him he views at me and smiles as Emily grasps my hand and pulls me to my feet "Maxie, this is my better half Kaitlyn. Kait, this is my older sibling Max."

I hold my hand out anticipating a conventional handshake, however he pushes it aside and gives me a warm embrace "no hands, we're family now." He takes a gander at me from a careful distance and gestures favorably "she's unquestionably an improvement from that stood up slapper you stuck yourself with for such a long time Emsie" I redden at this, as though she can detect my humiliation she folds her arm over my abdomen and presses her lips into my hair.

"Try not to be a thrower your entire life." She moans and presses me to her, habitually I slip a hand into her back pocket and barely care about it. "Will we proceed to observe some football before you figure out how to annoy everybody?" She asks with a giggle and them three take off from the house reciting a type of football melody together.

***

"That ref was a top of the line prick" Max gripes once more, hammering his lager glass on the bar table hard and sending a portion of the fluid slopping on the table.

"So you continue to state Maxie, it's done at this point. So shut up, cheer up and how about we become inebriated." Emily unsettles his hair prior to standing and reporting she's returning to the bar for another round. I would already be able to feel the impacts of the days drinking, my cheeks feel warm and there's a decent buzz in my mind making everything brilliantly interesting.

"She's the most joyful I've seen her in quite a while" Maxie says, freeing me once again from my own musings. I feel the become flushed spread across my cheeks at his words and I attempt to dodge his green eyes as they gaze at mine, so like his sisters. "You satisfy her."

I bite my lip and peer down at the table "she fulfills me" I state just, in light of the fact that it's actual.

"Emily revealed to me how you met initially, that must've been hard on you? She enlightened me concerning what Charlotte said to her and how she's lived with that lament for such a long time" he says delicately, contacting cover my hand with his "I'm happy you discovered each other once more." I gesture and grin at him, uncertain of what it is I'm intended to state.

Fortunately I don't have the opportunity to think excessively, on the grounds that Emily returns quickly with another plate of brews and shots and starts giving them out to us. She sits back close to me and spots her hand on my denim clad thigh and raises a shot glass with her free hand "to my older sibling Maxwell, best of luck getting hitched. I allow it a half year before you're well and really subservient to Amanda" she thumps her shot back and we take cues from her, the fluid consumes my throat in transit down making me rapidly wash the taste away with a significant piece of brew "all joking aside however, in case you're as content with her as I am with this one. You'll have an extraordinary life" she says as she watches me affectionately. That articulation makes my inner parts dissolve and I can't fight the temptation to close the distance among us and press my lips to hers modestly.

"Give it a rest Em, we've actually got my stag to appreciate and its absolutely impossible no doubt about it." Emily takes a gander at me prior to taking a gander at her sibling and shrugging her shoulders

"As much as I'd love to go through a night with you and your bone headed companions, I would prefer not to leave Kait all alone," I press her hand and intrude on her words.

"No chance, you're not blaming me. Go, I'll be fine." I praise her for needing to be with me, I would prefer not to actually be separated from her. In any case, I won't let her blame me so as to escape going out with her sibling. Emily takes a gander at me pleadingly, nearly like she needs me to denounce what I've quite recently said so she doesn't need to go, however I don't move.

Running her hands through her hair she takes a long beverage from her half quart glass lastly yields "fine, yet I'm not watching." Max's roaring chuckle sound out making a couple of different supporters investigate at our table and shake their heads disapprovingly. He drinks his lager at record speed and stands from the table.

"Indeed, as much as I'd love to remain here throughout the night I guaranteed Amanda I'd be home part way calm." Emily and I stand and he gives us each an embrace prior to disregarding us, Emily's hand takes mine and our fingers trim together right away. I grin bashfully at the lady close to me, who thus, comes to over with her free hand to fold a lock of hair behind my ear and afterward allows her fingers to trail across my cheek.

This straightforward stroke, so delicate and delicate, basically makes them murmur as I incline toward her fingers and let my eyes hang close "I love having you here" she mumbles making me open my eyes and watch her face. Her eyes are delicate as she looks at me, her lips transformed up into a little, sweet grin, making my heart avoid a beat.

I snatch her hand and carry it to my lips, ghosting them across her knuckles "I love being here. Much obliged to you for offering it to me."

Emily chuckles a little prior to shrugging her shoulders and completes her beverage in one go "you probably won't feel a similar route after we eat with my mom tomorrow, how about we go. I've been pondering stripping that shirt off of you throughout the day."

The look she gives makes me wriggle marginally in my seat before she pulls me to my feet and leads me out of the bar. Outside, she wraps her arm around my shoulder while I slide my hand into the back pocket of her pants, incapable to fight the temptation to press her firm ass somewhat. I feel Emily's breath on my ear as we walk gradually together "you truly shouldn't man handle me in broad daylight." I crush again and snicker dryly.

"Lady, in the event that I need to crush your rear end I will damn well press your butt" I need to accomplish something other than press her ideal ass, however we're openly and I would prefer not to get captured.

Clearly she has various thoughts however in light of the fact that subsequent to strolling a couple of more yards in a charged quietness, I end up being guided down the side of a type of shop. Emily moves me so my back is against the divider, her hands are propped against the block on one or the other side of my face, her lips scarcely a hairs expansiveness away. My hands pull her hips towards me and I shudder when she pushes against me immovably "you cause me to feel things I've never felt. I for the most part have very great poise, however with you it simply disappears" her lips press against mine delicately before she pulls back and lays her head on mine. "It's startling and great all simultaneously." Her lips brush mine once more, when I feel her attempt to pull away my hands get the front of her shirt firmly keeping her to me. Her hands move from being propped against the divider to holding my midriff firmly, her fingers delving in hard enough to nearly be agonizing. Our lips move couple together, our tongues participate, start a moderate, exotic dance. Lighting sparkles within me and causing every one of my muscles south of my midsection to hold delightfully.

She parts my legs with one of her thighs and presses it against my middle, with no idea I crush my hips down on it hard and groan against her mouth. Moving my hands from the front of her shirt to her hair, tangling in the delicate, sandy braids and holding her mouth to mine immovably. The hands she has on my midsection slip to my behind and she moves my hips against her once more, controlling the pressing factor and causing a heavenly and addictive grating with each pass.

We become a knot of limps, groans, jeans and pants together. Apparently not thinking often about being in a particularly open spot as our mouths move enthusiastically together and I'm squirming against her thigh with surrender.

The sound of a vehicle horn sounding out and about near to makes Emily pull away, flabbergasting me and flushed. My chest hurling as I attempt to recover some degree of poise "Em?" I figure out how to get out as I endeavor to control my fast heartbeat.

"Indeed dear?" She mumbles against my sanctuary.

"Take me to bed..." She says nothing more as she grasps my hand and leads me away, strolling back toward her dad's home at a snappy walk. The appearance of assurance all over would typically appear to be funny to me in the event that I didn't feel like I was going to soften into a sex starved puddle.

The moment the room entryway closes behind us, we're on one another. Dress flies toward each path as we strip each other hurriedly and breakdown onto the bed, finding every others lips right away. I push Emily on her back, riding her thighs and dissolve my mouth to hers covetously. She kisses me hard, her hands following down my front to my bosoms, squeezing my areolas immovably, moving them between her thumb and pointer, sending a sharp wound of delight race through me.

She sits upstanding so we're nose to nose, her lips never leaving mine, I feel her work day her legs somewhat under me, compelling my hips to rise. I fold my legs over her, carrying my body nearer to my darlings, savoring her glow and closeness. Coming to behind me, my fingers quickly start to search out her sex. It doesn't take long until I'm covered in her, knuckle profound, twisting my fingers round inside her.

Emily groans into my mouth and shakes her crotch against my hand prior to sliding her fingers down my stomach and driving them into me. The sensation of her filling me while I'm filling her is stunning. She imitates my activities, making my hips start finding a musicality with her hand. We moan and pant into our kiss as our fingers begin to move together.

I feel her inner parts start to hold around me as I start wavering on the edge of what I have no uncertainty will be the first of numerous climaxes this evening. "I need to accompany you" she groans against my lips, her hips shaking all over "I'm so close Kaitlyn."

Clenching down on her shoulder, my entire body hardens at her words as I clip down on her fingers, finding my delivery. Emily isn't a long ways behind, I pull back enough to see her lovely highlights wind as her climax rocks through her. Her stomach muscles fix and her head inclines back somewhat. She flounders back against the bed and takes a full breath, seeing her, the manner in which her chest flickers under the dainty covering of sweat that is accumulated there.

I need more, so sliding down I push her thighs open and lift them enough to rest them over my shoulders. Her sex sparkles with the proof of her excitement and I lick my lips at the sight. "What are you doing down there?" Emily husks out at me, I don't reply. Rather I take her in my mouth and run my tongue over the length of her gradually, tuning in to the sharp murmur of breath as it leaves her body. My eyes gaze toward her, watching her ideal face unwind as she feels my tongue whirl around her. "Goodness fuck..." she groans when I plunge my tongue down further, sliding it inside prior to hauling it back up and flicking the tip of her clit with it. Her hands tangle in my hair, holding me to her, managing me to where she needs me to be.

I move my tongue quicker, as I start sucking her into my mouth and battering the tip of her swollen clit with it. I love the manner in which Emily tastes, it's addictive and never neglects to cause me to let completely go when I have my head covered in the middle of her thighs. I'd spend forever here in the event that I found the opportunity.

I taste her peak before I feel her harden underneath me, the legs I have hung around my shoulder fix themselves around my neck prior to going leeway. I kiss my way up, waiting at her attractive hips prior to kissing my way up her stomach and chest and moving off of her. I pull her to me, enclosing her by my arms and she nestles into my neck "allow me a moment, my bones feel like jam" she mumbles into my skin making me chuckle.

"I fail to remember it should be difficult for you to keep up. You know with me being youthful and spritely and you being old and agreeable" I bother, Emily breathes out boisterously and shakes her head unfortunately.

"Well you've done it now..." it takes me a second to understand shouldn't something be said about's to occur, yet I'm too moderate since I wind up stuck under her with my hands held down firmly over my head, leaving me vulnerable to her. Emily floats above me, an energetic grin all the rage "any final words Ms. Suarez?"

I make a gesture of blowing a kiss at her and smile "simply that I love you" her lips push down on mine and I can feel her grin.

"Great, cause I love you" she answers subsequent to breaking our kiss and ghosting her lips down my neck to my chest.

***

I don't think I've ever felt as awkward as I do well presently, staying here in an upscale tapas eatery with Emily and her mom and it's obvious to see that the two ladies couldn't be more extraordinary and the reasonable hatred they have for one another is discernible. Emily is sat to one side, straightforwardly opposite her mom, and I'm happy for her closeness. Any time the discussion takes a turn that makes me feel awkward or whenever I'm dependent upon one of Elizabeth's testing addresses Emily intertwines my hand with hers and gives it a consoling press.

"So Kaitlyn, where in America are you from?" Elizabeth asks as she takes a taste of cool white wine from her glass. Gulping the food in my mouth, I make an honest effort to seem loose yet it's troublesome when my heart is dashing.

"Texas, Houston Texas Ma'am. Brought up." I attempt to sound certainty however my voice comes out a tranquil mumble, Emily's mom maintains eye contact with me. Her virus blue eyes gazing into mine.

"Where are your family from? They're not American I expect?"

"Mother! Truly?" Emily intrudes on, I pat her hand with mine and grin at her.

"Em, it's fine." Turning back to the lady before me, my grin is somewhat more sure this time as I forge ahead "no, they're American residents. They got citizenship some time prior. Yet, they moved from Puerto Rico with my two sisters. I'm the one in particular that was brought into the world in the states. My mother was pregnant with me before they moved."

She tightens her lips a little and gestures favorably at my answer "fascinating. I envision you talk they're primary language as well? It probably been difficult for them to become familiar with a subsequent language." I need to fight the temptation to feign exacerbation at her tone, yet oversee and give myself a psychological congratulatory gesture.

I feel Emily's hand lay on my thigh, I investigate and see her entire body is tense and grin a little to myself prior to responding to Elizabeth's inquiry "sí, hablan buen inglés pero en casa tasks hablamos español." Emily splutters into her water glass as she chuckles at my answer and she goes to take a gander at me affectionately, the grin all the rage irresistible as I grin back at her.

"I guess that teaches me a lesson for posing such countless inquiries, pardon me. Emily was with Charlotte for quite a while, beautiful young lady, great family. Did you actually meet her?" This overwhelms me a little and I gesture.

"Once, at school. However, it was so short I don't actually consider it a gathering." By this point I can feel the dissatisfaction vibrate off of Emily, her grasp on my leg fixes and I see her other hand hold into a clench hand.

I connect and put a hand at the back out her neck, and I don't mind her opinion, her hairs maneuvered into a free bun yet my fingers go through the delicate, short hairs that have come free. I feel her loosen up somewhat however she's tense as she frowns at the one who brought forth her, her jaw is held into a tight line as she talks "mum, for somebody who professes to be so shrewd, you express some genuinely moronic things now and again."

"Emily..." I start yet she cuts me off with a look and my mouth snaps shut.

Elizabeth takes a gander at her girl with a virus gaze and spots the edge of her mouth with a napkin "I don't have a clue what you mean, I was making discussion. What's the issue?"

"The issue is that you're inquiring as to whether she ever met my ex. The ex who left me by the path in the wake of getting me through four years of wretchedness when she moved out to the states. She's wedding another person and I've never been more joyful. I love Kaitlyn. Become acclimated to that."

"Well she will be at the wedding, did you realize that? Charlotte will be there." This is unmistakably news to Emily as she looks bothered and takes a gander at me prior to gazing back at her mom.

"So? She'll be there with her new life partner, shouldn't be astonished seeing as he went to class with Max they're still companions. I'll be there with Kaitlyn, for what reason does it make a difference?"

Elizabeth flags a server for the check and starts assembling her things, as she sets her Visa on the table she sets me with a look of objection and presses together her lips "I'm certain you're stunning Kaitlyn, however I've generally needed the best for my kids. They went to the best schools, each are running after acceptable professions and I needed the best counterparts for them in relationships." She stops before she takes a gander at Emily "I never needed this for you, yet I became acclimated to the possibility of your... specific tastes. Charlotte was all around reared, from a decent family and had a well-rounded schooling. She was preferred for you over this... American."

"Hey..." I start to protest yet Emily intertwines my hand with hers and cuts me off suddenly.

In the wake of trading a look with me, she goes to her mom and takes a quieting breath "I will say this one time, so you need to hear what I'm stating and become accustomed to it. Else, you may find that you see even less of me later on." I ribbon my fingers through hers, I can determine what she needs to state isn't simple and I need to attempt and quietly show her that I'll

128

uphold her through this. "I began to look all starry eyed at another lady five years prior, I went gaga for this lady." She holds my hand up prior to allowing them to lay back on the table "Charlotte knew how I believed, I was straightforward with her however she settled on me settle on a decision. I settled on some unacceptable decision. I quit adoring Charlotte quite a while before I met Kait however ended up making a cursory effort with her. Mother, we will be together however long she needs me. So quit pushing your vainglorious thoughts on what or who you figure I ought to be and just left me alone content with the lady I love?"

Elizabeth looks among Emily and I and shakes her head "be upbeat Emily, yet don't think this is me giving you my approval using any and all means" and with those words, she leaves.

Emily and I sit peacefully briefly, her hand remains tight in mine and I keep my fingers running calming designs against the rear of her neck. As the quiet delays between us, I end up needing to break it, yet I don't have a clue what I'm intended to state in the present circumstance. I open my mouth a couple of times to state something, state anything, yet each time I wind up snapping it shut again as I watch the agony move quickly over her face making my heart hurt for her. "I'm sorry you needed to see that" she murmurs at last, waking up me from my quiet.

I take her face in both of my hands and go her to see me "absolutely never apologize about others, you cautioned me something to that effect would occur" I scan her green eyes for an indication of how she's inclination. Emily murmurs and leans her temple against mine, I can hear her taking a progression of full breaths before she thinks back up and offers me a little grin. It's a helpless impersonation of her standard grin however, not contacting her eyes, her whole body is tense and I'd give anything at that time to remove the disappointment from her. "What's experiencing your head Em?" I ask, not certain I need to hear the appropriate response.

I keep my palms on her cheeks, compelling all her eyes on me "I don't have the foggiest idea. I don't have the foggiest idea why I hoped for something else from her. I'm distraught that she brought Charlotte up like that and before you stop me, you merit a statement of regret. On the off chance that not from me, at that point one for my mom's sake. I'm so screwing furious she talked about you like that, similar to you were underneath her." A little grin plays all the rage, one that contacts her eyes and I loosen up a bit "you dealt with her well however, when she got some information about communicating in Spanish and you fundamentally set her in her proper place inconspicuously." I feel adequately great to drop my hands from her face to accept both of hers as I shrug.

"I had a lot of training first year when I needed to continue to take care of you" Emily giggles at this and I grin at the sound, she sounds practically joyful. She inclines forward and kisses the tip of my nose daintily prior to standing up and pulling me to my feet.

"How about we go, we actually need to get you a dress and I told father we wouldn't be late."

Chapter eight: Thinking for all to hear

Observing Emily remaining close to her sibling as he trades promises with his better half to be makes my heart beat increment ten times. She's wearing what must be a bespoke, hand crafted suit that embraces every one of her bends and praises the one her sibling and his groomsmen. Seeing her makes my mouth dry, how the fuck did I deal with get so fortunate?

She continues to grab my attention across the congregation and glimmers me a shrewd smile prior to turning her consideration back to what in particular's going on close to her. She situated me with her Dad and his folks who, similar to their child, have invited me thoughtfully. Her mum is sat on similar column of seats as us however has given a valiant effort to try not to need to really recognize my reality yet that is more than alright by me.

Toward the finish of the function I wind up lingering around outside alone, trusting that Emily will discover me so we can get a taxi to the gathering. The late-spring sun is warm on my skin as I tilt my face up somewhat to relax in the warm beams gleaming down. Different visitors are blending near and grin sympathetic at me when they pass, a portion of Emily's family stop to make proper acquaintance and I present myself as her better half which sends a little rush through me each time the word gets away from my lips.

Arms winding around my midriff surprises me somewhat before I recollect who's arms they are and I quickly unwind into the lady behind me. "Along these lines, there's this young lady I'm here with and she's overall quite all. In any case, you're simply too ravishing to even think about resisting, extravagant a snappy snog before she gets me?" I jeer and pivot in my lady friends arms and set her with disliking gaze "gracious poop, didn't understand it was you Kaitlyn." She puckers her lips at me and starts making kissy commotions making me chuckle. I simply slap her shoulder prior to hanging my arms around her neck.

"Should've realized you'd be a player" I joke, coming to up to kiss her cheek "all joking aside, you look so screwing hot in this suit." I murmur as my hands drop down to get a handle on the lapels on her coat "I endorse enormously."

The look I get after I state that makes me powerless at the knees "all things considered, on the off chance that you do your best, you'll will see me out of it as well" she shuts that off with a wink and I can't resist the urge to get a handle all over in my grasp and pull her lips to mine so I can kiss her avariciously. She pulls away excessively fast for my preferring and I frown at her to ensure she realizes I'm disappointed making her giggle "quit sulking it's unsuitable, I have photograph's to go profess to appreciate participating in." When she inclines in near my ear I feel a moderate shudder spread down my spine "and that implies in the event that I've gotta go have my image taken do as well, you. Please." She gets a handle on my hand and pulls me reluctantly to where her sibling and his new spouse are representing photos.

I do my piece of remaining by Emily when I'm asked as well, and watching her posture and grin when she's remained with her sibling and her folks. I love watching her, the manner in which she moves with a simple elegance has consistently boggled me. In any case, despite the fact that I'm lost in viewing my better half mess about with her sibling I'm hit with a staggering inclination that I'm being viewed. It's an unusual sensation, the

133

hairs on the rear of my neck prickle and the hair on my arms remain on end.

I don't have long to harp on it however in light of the fact that I'm rapidly re-joined by Emily who brushes her lips against mine and folds an arm over my midriff "we should get a taxi and head off to the gathering. I'm prepared for a lager." Despite the standard feeling of wellbeing I feel when Emily's nearby I actually feel a little anxious and my eyes continue to flick around the hordes of different visitors "everything alright dear?"

I gesture and gaze toward her "better believe it, I just... sense that somebody's gazing at me? Is that peculiar?"

Emily shrugs and presses her lips to my sanctuary "not when you look tantamount to you do, no." I watch her glance around and her face falls marginally "yet Charlotte is gazing at us..." She gestures with her head toward a short brunette who has her eyes bolted all over, when our eyes meet my skin prickles with anxiety. Emily presses my abdomen, directing my consideration, I figure out how to draw my consideration from her ex and gaze upward into the eyes I worship "don't stress over her, recollect that I'm with you. Like I ought to be" her fingers from her free hand trail delicately across my jaw and she pecks me softly on the lips "presently please, I need a beverage."

***

On the dancefloor couples move around us, I'm enveloped with Emily's arms, her cheek leaning against mine as we dance gradually to the music playing all through the room. "You know," I mutter as we influence together, our bodies squeezed so intently there isn't an inch of room between us "the last time we moved together, it was so exceptional, yet it was so dismal simultaneously." Emily's arms fix around me and her lips contact my cheek.

She pulls her face away to take a gander at me, her lips twisting up into a delicate grin "I know, yet it's distinctive at this point. I don't feel regretful for not having any desire to leave you, I can allow myself to adore you the manner in which I need to."

"Also, how is that?"

She smiles and kisses me tenderly "asides from the self-evident? Nodding off and awakening close to you consistently, sharing the little minutes that mean the most. Calling you first when something great occurs or realizing that when something poo goes down that I'll see you by the day's end and you'll sit and talk it through with me until you're upbeat my heads in a decent space." I feel my inner parts go to goo at her words, I love it when I see this side of her. "Furthermore, the sex is well better

135

than expected as well so that is likewise a reward!" She snickers when I slap her arm, however she takes steps to pull me near her and kisses me immovably on the mouth.

"You're such an ass now and then!" I whine, not under any condition frantic, however I can't let her see that.

"Would you need me some other way?"

I eccentricity and eyebrow a shake my head "unquestionably not."

As the melody reaches a conclusion and changes into something more up-beat, Emily gets a handle on my hand in hers and leads me off the dancefloor "how about we have another beverage and afterward we can go. I need to get you out of that dress" at that I basically drag her toward the bar, a lady on a mission, it's not until I see a couple of blue eyes that I stop.

Before me is Charlotte, taking a gander at me in what must be perceived as weariness before her eyes move over to Emily and her appearance mellow. I need to slap that look off of her pompous face however I don't. Rather I move so my back is flush against Emily's front and feel my internal parts warm when she folds her arms over my midsection.

Charlotte's eyes move among Emily and I in an interesting, confounded kind of path before she at long last chooses to speak "Emily, sweetheart. How are you?" I harden marginally at the charm however Emily basically strokes my stomach with her thumb and I unwind somewhat. How is it she has such a quieting impact over me?

"Charlotte, I'm acceptable much obliged. You recall Kaitlyn?" Charlotte takes a gander at me and presses together her lips.

"No, can't state I review you. My expressions of remorse." I shake my head and grin as heartily as Possible.

"Forget about it, we just met once and it was some time prior." I marshal, as courteous as I can bear.

Quiet falls over the three of us, I start to stress my base lip with my teeth, it's hard for me not having the option to peruse Emily's face. I don't have a clue her opinion, how she's inclination. The solitary solace I have is the glow of her body near me, the relieving cadence of her thumb rehashing a similar way over the smooth material of my dress "Emily, do you figure we could talk. Alone briefly?" Again, Charlotte looks among us however overlooks my essence.

"No, anything you need to state you can say before Kait." Emily's tone is cool and shy, I remember it to the one she so regularly used to recognize me in the beginning of our kinship. Before there was any kinship.

Settling on a brief instant choice I venture out of Emily's grasp and lay a hand on her shoulder "no, thumbs up and talk. I'll go get us a few beverages, another brew infant, yes?" Her green eyes lock on my dim earthy colored ones and she maintains eye contact with me, in that one look I'm attempting to disclose to her I confide in her. That I love her, I simply trust she gets that before I dismiss and stroll from both of them.

I need to remain quiet about rehashing that she cherishes me, that she needs to be with me while I stand by at the bar to get served. I at last request another lager and a glass of wine and incline toward the cool oak bar, my eyes filtering the room. Chills course through me, regardless of the warm air flowing the room. "Everything alright Kaitlyn?" Marks voice takes me leap, gripping my chest with a hand I give him a little grin and gesture.

"Better believe it, I'm acceptable. It's been a delightful day. You should be glad?" I ask, attempting to move the subject away from me.

He grins, a perfect representation of the one I've seen so often all the rage "indeed, I hear you had a remarkable spat with Emily's mom?"

I feign exacerbation at that and he giggles noisily, motioning for the barkeep while I take a beverage of my wine "you could state that, she left unexpectedly. Her splitting words were something along the lines of 'be upbeat yet you don't have my approval' from the manner in which she was talking I don't know whether her most serious issue is the reality I'm American or if this is on the grounds that I'm a lady?" I snicker with Mark as he blends the scotch in his glass marginally prior to taking a taste.

"Knowing Liz, it's likely both. Where is my dear girl in any case?" He glances around as though anticipating that she should by one way or another marvelously show up since he's acknowledged she isn't anywhere near.

Taking another significant piece of wine for some fluid fortitude, I disregard the sickness in my stomach and deal with the most real grin I can "we ran into Charlotte, she needed to converse with Emily. I demanded they do only it, so here I am." I hold my hands out and watch as his eyes limited somewhat, with a shake of his head he takes another significant piece of the golden alcohol in his glass.

"She's a dreadful bit of work that one. I never enjoyed her." This overwhelms me and it should peruse obviously all over as he smiles and proceeds "the manner in which she controlled Emily, drove her on for over ten years. Ten years of my girl's life was constrained by that young lady. She lost the flash she once had the year she went out to the States, it wasn't until she got back home for Christmas her last year in New York that I really saw it return."

I see him baffled briefly, considering what in heaven's name it is he's discussing. And afterward it hits me, the sincere we had in the café that night, the charge between us. Flagging the adjustment in our relationship, the apparently guiltless kiss on the cheek and the consistent informing during winter break that year. "I recollect that year, I believe Emily." And I mean it, I do confide in her "on the off chance that those two expected to talk, at that point I'm satisfied with giving them the space they may require" I think.

Imprint gestures and purges his glass, motioning for the barkeep again he arranges us both a beverage. My backs went to the remainder of the room when I feel a hand on my shoulder, without hoping to see who it is I reach up and interface my fingers through hers "beginning and end alright?" I ask, still not pivoting.

Emily pulls on my shoulder giving me no decision except for to see her "I'm so..." I press a finger to her lips immovably and shake my head, recognizing easily the dissatisfaction she's inclination at this time.

"Try not to, would you like to go?" I ask discreetly, moving my fingers from her ideal lips to the rear of her neck. Disregarding her dad behind me and every other person in the room as I pull her mouth to mine and meet her lips in a delicate grasp. At the point when she at long last pulls away and sees me there's a decided look in her eye, her jaw is set in a tight line, yet she gestures.

I remain back while she bids farewell to her loved ones however we leave together connected at the hip and bounce straight into the rear of a holding up taxi. The ride home hushes up, I continue finding her taking a gander at me with an odd demeanor painted across her face yet I don't scrutinize her. Regardless of her quietness, I don't feel stressed or apprehensive, the manner in which her hand is in mine and hanging on firmly stops any questions the more suspicious piece of me would need to rest. Rather I locate a mitigating quiet from her touch and lean my head against her shoulder, allowing my eyes to close.

"Kaitlyn, infant we're home" Emily's lips are squeezed against my ear, the delicate thunder of the taxis motor as it sits inert outside of the house. I flicker a couple of times as I accumulate my heading yet permit Emily to help me out of the vehicle and up and into the house.

We dress for bed in a similar calm we sat in the rear of the taxi prior, any sexual expectation consuming between us prior at night had disseminated. Yet, I couldn't care less, I simply need to feel her near me around evening time.

We lie in bed next to each other, our countenances simply inches separated. Emily's hands are running here and there my sides gradually "would you like to discuss it?" I murmur.

Her hand stills briefly prior to continuing its delicate ministration against my ribs "yes and no. I'm battling to perceive any reason why I went through ten years of my existence with that individual." I can make out the dislike her wonderful face through the murkiness and lift my hand to smooth the wrinkle between her temples.

"I'm certain I've advised you before that on the off chance that you continue to scowl you'll get wrinkles, and you're excessively beautiful for that." Emily giggles dryly prior to pulling me closer to her, bringing my body against hers "what happened infant?"

142

"Ugh, what do you think? She went on this entire digression about how she had been a numbskull to discard such countless years, that she'd addressed mum and she'd informed her concerning meeting you and how mum believes she's better for me." Emily tenses close to me as I attempt to overlook the beating in my ears "when I revealed to her that I wasn't intrigued. That I was content with the individual I should've been with five years prior and would you like to understand what her reaction to that was?" I gesture, not confiding in my voice now "she said that when she came out to America that week, she really came out to say a final farewell to me after graduation. She said that when she saw our little trade at the bistro she could see something had occurred and that is the point at which she chose to disclose to me she was moving out. At that point she saw us moving, perceived how close we were and that established it for her. It wasn't the way that she needed me to focus on our relationship, she simply didn't need any other person to have me. She removed a long time from us." I let my breath out in a long moan and shake my head marginally attempting to gather the haze up. "Kait, would i be able to ask you something... furthermore, I need you to be straightforward."

"Anything" I react absent a lot of thought, since I realize I'd disclose to her anything she needed to hear.

"Where do you think we'd be currently in the event that we'd gotten together back, at that point?" She murmurs this at me through the murkiness and for once, rather than simply noting hastily, I pause for a minute to think about my answer. To give her the trustworthiness I disclosed to her she'd get.

Where might we be on the off chance that we hadn't lost the most recent five years because of somebody's unimportance, I close my eyes and let the picture wash over me; Sitting in the front room of our shared house, Emily, still in her residency, returns home after a long move and sits with me as we open and offer a jug of wine. I'd request us take out as we observed some garbage on television, examining our day. I'd attempt and stay aware of what she's truism yet I'd be excessively entranced by the development of her lips to truly comprehend what it is she's maxim.

We'd have supper together and head to sleep together, have intercourse and nod off wrapped up together. Ordinary everyday things, aside from, she wouldn't be my sweetheart, she'd be my better half.

At the point when I open my eyes I see Emily watching me intently, I lean a hand against her cheek and run my nose along the length of hers "I think, we'd be living respectively and presumably wedded. I'd need that since I need an existence with you."

"I was trusting you'd state that since I've been thinking, when we return to New York. How might you feel if the entirety of our things were in a similar space, you realize one we'd share together, rather than paying rent on two shoe box lofts?"

"Emily Forester are you requesting that I move in with you?" I jest, my heart thumping quickly.

"Truly, that is actually the thing I'm inquiring."

"At that point we would do well to begin searching for a greater loft I presume." Emily pushes me back against the bed, my thighs part effectively for her and she holds her weight above me with her elbows squeezed against the bed.

"I love you" she murmurs prior to pushing her lips to mine energetically "it's constantly been you."

Chapter nine: Home

Figuring out how to impart a space to Emily is potentially perhaps the simplest change I've ever needed to make. Learning every one of her subtleties and propensities has been intriguing; like the manner in which she takes her shoes and socks off the moment she gets in on the grounds that she despises wearing them. Or then again how she'll secure herself in the restroom the moment she returns home if she's had an unpleasant day at work, those days are the hardest, cajoling her out or sitting on the virus floor tiles with her until she's prepared to discuss it. There was one night where I discovered her remaining in the shower completely dressed under the water, she'd been in there so long the water had run cold. That evening was one of the hardest, for the two of us, seeing her so beat up and removed about something made meextremely upset. In any case, generally it's been beyond what I might envision.

In the most recent year of being together we've had a lot of contentions, I swear that lady gets more difficult as she gets more established. Yet, the battles simply compare to make up sex and that truly is the awesome.

"Thus, what you're stating Emily is that you're dropping our date around evening time. Despite the fact that it's our commemoration?" I ask, feeling surrendered as I sit at my little work area in my make move office at work. Mobile phone to my ear while my free hand rubs hovers on my sanctuary.

"Not by decision dear, I got pursued somewhere around one of the medical clinics chairmen and I have a half year of graphing to do. Evidently none of them have my mark and they all need marking before tomorrow." She moans, obviously exasperated, I realize it isn't her issue yet I can't reject that I'm baffled. We've had this gotten ready for around two months.

I take a quieting breath and pull out my work organizer "we'll need to reschedule then I presume. What time do you think you'll be home this evening?" Silence, that is rarely a decent sign. I stand by quietly briefly prior to rehashing myself "simply reveal to me Emily."

"Genuinely? I'm presumably going to be here throughout the evening so I won't be home till tomorrow." I can hear the strain in her voice, as much I love her, I scorn offering her to her work some of the time and she knows this. "I truly am sorry infant. I have the entire end of the week off however so we'll accomplish something at that point, I guarantee."

"Better believe it, sure. I'll call you later." I realize I sound inaccessible, I can hear the disappointment in my own voice.

"Alright. I love you?" The manner in which she says that resembles she's posing an inquiry as opposed to advising me, measuring my response and I scorn that she believes she needs to do that.

"I love you. I'll call later I guarantee." Emily separates the call at that and I discharge a perceptible moan and lean forward until my brow hits the strong wood of my work area.

"Inconvenience in heaven?" The sound of Gregory's voice alarms me, yet insufficient to make me need to lift my head away from the wood surface and out of this funk I feel myself falling into. I hear the delicate strides of my manager as he strolls towards me and pulls out one of the seats I have at the contrary side of my work area. "What's going on Kaitlyn?" His voice is delicate and I have a sense of security enough to lift my head marginally to set him with a melancholy gaze.

"Emily needs to work around evening time." Sitting back I set my hands in my lap and watch as Gregory works out what that implies.

"Gracious, isn't today you're commemoration?"

"That's right. However, rather she will be at the emergency clinic." I clarify, irritation unmistakable in my voice.

Gregory pushes his wire rimmed glasses to the highest point of his head and folds his legs "gracious dear, she stuck in a medical procedure or something?" This isn't the first run through Emily's work has meddled with our arrangements, and as a rule Gregory's one of the principal individuals I vent to when I get calls like the one I've recently gotten.

Feigning exacerbation I squirm with a portion of the papers around my work area and shake my head "if just it was that intriguing, she has graphs to sign or something." I watch as Gregory measures that data and glares a bit.

"So what's preventing you from bringing your sweet little ass down there and I don't have a clue, astonishing her?"

"Indeed, I don't have the foggiest idea. I've never done that, imagine a scenario in which she doesn't need me there."

"Pfft, she's presumably more irritated about missing around evening time than you are. Take her some food and I don't know be with her?" I take a gander at him mindfully, my teeth start gnawing at the edge of my base lip "look, it's your decision to

149

make toward the day's end, however you're benefiting neither of you in any way by staying here pouting." With those splitting words my bashful manager brushes down his jeans prior to standing and disregarding me once more. Getting a pencil I tap it against the work area, he's makes a valid statement. What is preventing me from simply going to the medical clinic and seeing her? Would she need to see me while she was grinding away? It's something I've never done, I've never had motivation to. Yet, a year after we originally chanced upon one another in the Emergency Room, it nearly appears to be fitting.

Psyche made up I check my watch, our table was reserved for seven and it's a brief time after five at this point. I make a psychological arrangement and rapidly assemble my assets before I can lose face and advance out of the theater.

***

"No, I don't have an arrangement. I simply need to see her for five minutes, would you be able to reveal to me where I can discover her?" I ask the assistant for what feels like the 20th time.

"I'm grieved, however without an arrangement I can't permit you through." The receptionists tone is cut as her eyes take in my fatigued appearance, I feign exacerbation and am going to pull out my PDA when a natural voice sounds from behind me.

"Kaitlyn, what are you doing here?" I go to see Emily strolling across the hall, I failed to remember how great she glances in scours. The pale dark material hangs freely over her body, however with her white coat and stethoscope sticking around her neck she looks each piece like something from my dirtiest dreams. I make a sound as if to speak and venture forward to kiss her cheek, the nerves thick in my stomach.

For what reason am I so apprehensive? Emily looks befuddled as I remain before her, take out pack close by and a little grin all the rage "indeed, I er, I figured since you're not in medical procedure and said you will sign diagrams throughout the evening. You'd need to eat? What's more, since you were unable to make it to supper I figured..." I trail off, my eyes fixed on the floor, too terrified to even think about looking at her and face the dismissal I know is coming.

I feel Emily's fingers twist under my jawline as she powers my eyes up to meet hers "so you figured you carry supper to me?" I gesture and watch as she grins splendidly at me and grasps my hand "that is splendid. Please" I follow her obediently as she drives me through the twisting passageways of the emergency clinic to one of the lifts. Squeezing the call button, we stand next to each other while we pause. I'm baffled to see it's practically full when it opens, yet this doesn't hinder Emily, she pulls me in by the hand directing me towards the back where she arranges me before her while she holds me by the hips.

I wheeze when I feel her delinquent fingers travel under my shirt, following the touchy skin simply over the belt of my pants setting my skin ablaze. Emily's nose is covered in my hair, her bosoms press against my back and despite the fact that I can't see her face, I know she's grinning. Concealed toward the edge of the packed lift, it feels like there's a static charged air pocket encompassing us.

All to soon the lift stops at our floor and Emily's fingers move from that delicate fix of skin to the little of my back as she manages me out and back through another arrangement of passageways until she acquires me to a stop front of an entryway "it's not much, yet it's the lone spot in this grisly emergency clinic that you can complete anything" she clarifies as she bobbles with the entryway handle prior to opening it and demonstrating me into a faint stay with a bunch of lofts and a chaotic and jumbled work area.

Emily moves rapidly and starts pushing administrative work around the work area, arranging them into heaps. The disorder makes me grin a little, it's so not normal for the perfect monstrosity I live with that I peculiarity an eyebrow and gesture at the work area "in this way, it shows up you're very minimal chaotic?" Emily chuckles and rubs the rear of her neck, at the same time taking a gander at me with a timid grin.

"Something to that effect, sit. What did you bring me?" She eyes the sack insatiably as I sit at the extra seat at the work area and start discharging it. Compartments fill the work area alongside plastic cutlery and two jugs of lager.

"All things considered, I went to La Scala and revealed to them we wouldn't have been requiring our booking" Emily's pitiful look stops my words and I feign exacerbation at her blame ridden articulation, inclining forward I kiss her nose and shake my head "don't see me like that, it's fine I get it. Anyway, I requested some take out. All your #1 dishes. I figured we could eat and afterward I could assist you with getting of these so you may get an opportunity to really get back home for a couple of hours."

Emily's grin makes my heart shudder, even now I don't think I'll actually become acclimated to her grinning for me like that. It never neglects to turn me soft within, she grasps my hand and carries it to her lips, putting delicate kisses on the rear of every one of my fingers prior to kissing me immovably on the rear of my hand. "You," she stops to kiss my wrist "are the most superb," another delay as her lips press against the highest point of my arm "smart," her lips phantom across my shoulder and I shudder under the stroke "and kind lady I've ever met" her lips are on my cheek and take moderate actions until they discover their way to my holding up my mouth where she kisses me gradually, stirring up the moderate copying fire that is working in my gut.

It takes every last bit of resolution I have not to push her onto one of the beds behind us and show her exactly the amount I love her, rather I return her kiss briefly prior to pulling ceaselessly and setting her with a grin "will we eat?"

***

"I actually can't really accept that you can fashion my mark" she says as we stroll through the entryway of our shared condo "I mean I can, yet you do it so well!" I chuckle at this and disregard my jacket prior to hanging it up in the storage room and moving to the kitchen where Emily's as of now opening us each a brew.

Inclining toward the entryway I watch her move around the kitchen with a similar simple beauty I've generally respected, she stops to pull her shoes and socks off, tossing the socks into the hamper kept by the washer prior to pivoting and spotting me watching her "like what you see?" She asks with a wink, I giggle and shrug my shoulders.

"It's alright I surmise" I walk nearer so I can fold my arms over her midsection and nestle her neck "much better very close" I finish prior to nipping at her ear. Emily's arms are soon around my own midsection as she looks down at me affectionately, her lips pulled up into a little grin "what are you grinning at?" I mumble, fixing my hold on her.

Her hands raise up to my face, driving endlessly stray hairs before the backs of her fingers trail down my cheeks "you, us. One year together, I never figured it would occur. Fortunately, you're failure to try not to thump individuals on their arses..."

"I was the one being thumped down that time" I contend weakly making Emily giggle noisily at me, kissing my nose as she shakes her head.

"Subtleties, I'm happy it allowed me to compensate for some recent setbacks." She waggles her eyebrows interestingly at me and I snicker "in a greater number of ways than one on the off chance that you get my meaning" really trying to understand I push her against the counter prior to softening my lips against hers. At the point when I pull away her eyes are torching into mine, desire filled and splendid making my legs go feeble.

"Em?" I ask discreetly.

155

"Indeed my adoration?"

"Take me to bed." Before the final word has even left my mouth she lifts me up into her arms and starts advancing towards our room, stopping just to squeeze her lips immovably against mine. I hung tight quite a while for this, however it merited each second. Since now, with her, I'm the place where I should be. I'm home.

Epilog - after two years

"Gracious blessed fuck" I groan for all to hear prior to peering down and seeing Emily's head covered between my legs, I'll never feel sick of seeing this sight. The affection for my life acquiring me delight ways no one but she can. My whole body ignites with excitement as I feel her tongue cover somewhere within me "there, poo, not too far off" coming to down and tangling my hand in her dazzling light hair and holding her set up.

My hips pound persevering against Emily's tongue as I start scaling the heavenly path to orgasmic euphoria, and I for one can't stand by to arrive. At the point when my peak hits me, each muscle in my body gets, my hands fix in her hair holding her set up. I need her to stop and continue to go at the same time as she keeps lapping ceaselessly at my sex insatiably until I can presently don't take any more.

I constrain her mouth away from me and pull her lips to mine so I can kiss her eagerly, tasting myself on her as her tongue works its way into my mouth, moving exotically against mine until she pulls away and as usual, leaves me needing more. "You will be the passing of me" I gripe pitifully as my head leans against her shoulder, my hair adheres to my face in sweat-soaked braids which she drives away prior to squeezing her lips to my temple.

"What befell so much discussion about me staying aware of a more youthful lady?" I giggle weakly and turn my head to kiss her shoulder.

"That changed when I turned 26. I'm authoritatively old." I whine once more, more conviction in my voice powers a chuckle from the lady close to me. My eyes move before I turn over and prop myself up on my elbows and set her with a hard gaze "don't snicker at me Emily, I'm not kidding." Emily chomps her lip and ridicules a self-reproachful gaze prior to pulling me down on top of her and kissing me savagely.

"Three years Kait, would you be able to trust it?" I cuddle into her chest and smile foolishly at the prospect of having had the option to consider Emily dig throughout the previous three years.

"It's more acceptable now you don't have that stick forever wedged up your can yes." I laugh prior to transforming my head up to investigate her green eyes who are taking a gander at me unamused "no, I can barely handle it and I'm grateful for consistently I get with you" my fingers follow the state of the lips I've kissed multiple times, retaining their shape and bends as she grins down at me.

"How's your day been dear?" Emily asks me via telephone as I advance up from the metro, Emily has had an uncommon three day weekend and by its hints hasn't left the loft.

I murmur and evade different suburbanites as I walk energetically through the city roads "occupied, we're changing the play bill and Gregory's been a genuine annoyance throughout the day about it. However, I ought to be home in a short time so I'll see you at that point."

Emily falls quiet briefly before she talks "truly, great. Ten minutes. I'll see you then sweetheart." I hang up and push my hands in my jacket pocket, this is consistently the most noticeably awful piece of my drive home from work. Particularly today when I'm so restless about returning home to see Emily, she's been acting a little peculiar throughout the day. Messaging more than expected, calling more frequently than she normally would and afterward going all tranquil and far off the more extended the day goes on. I know she's planning some mischief, however I simply don't have the foggiest idea what.

I use the stairwell up to the condo rapidly, my psyche turning through the many different situations happening in my mind, every one more grievous than the last. As I remain outside the entryway, enters close by, I pause for a minute for myself. Preparing myself for whatever it is that is available for me when I stroll in, with a full breath and a long moan I open the entryway. It's anything but difficult to state that what I saw when I strolled through the entryway, is something I never expected in 1,000,000 years.

Each surface, counter, table, even the floor; was covered with roses. They were in jars, bushels, blessing packs, dazzling bunches of the new red blossoms embellished the condo. Candles consumed close by these, many them consuming together, making a warm brilliant shine around our home. The smell of cooking, flame wax and roses attacked my nose and along with what I was taking a gander at caused tears to consume in my ears and my breath get in the rear of my throat.

Pivoting the corner, the view I'm welcomed with makes me wheeze perceptibly. Emily is bowed on the floor, wearing a flawlessly customized suit, a solitary rose in one hand and a dark velvet box in the other. Her eyes are brilliant as she watches my response, her grin blinding as I take everything in and attempt to get my mind to see precisely the thing it is that is going on this moment. "Hey delightful," she says effectively, like this entire scene is something that happens each day.

"Howdy yourself" I murmur, my eyes wide and my mouth dry "what's happening?"

Emily makes a sound as if to speak and movements for me to come nearer, I oblige and feel her intertwine my hand with hers in the wake of dropping the rose she's holding "each day I get with you resembles a disclosure, these most recent three years have been the most awesome aspect my life and I have you and only you to thank for that." She stops as she swallows thickly and calmly inhales to pull it together "I love you, more than I've ever cherished anybody. You're the individual I need to gain my most joyful experiences with and the individual I need close by when things get unpleasant." Dropping my hand adequately long to open the crate in her grasp to show me an excellent single precious stone set in a white gold band "will you wed me?"

I gesture quietly, watching the grin all over broaden, the look in her eyes urges me to discover my voice "yes," I drop to my knees before her and take her face in my grasp, at long last confiding in my voice to sound fairly ordinary "yes," I kiss her lips solidly and feel the first of my tears tumble down my cheek.

Emily pulls back and slips the ring on the third finger of my left hand and sees it like she's seeing tone unexpectedly. Her eyes gobble up to mine and augment as though the truth of what's simply happened has just barely set in "you said yes?"

I gesture and grin brilliantly "I said yes." I'm not exactly ready for Emily handling me to the ground and sticking me underneath her. Her mouth discovers mine effectively and she kisses me with sincere, when her tongue follows my lip I can't battle the groan that gets away from me. She peers down at me adoringly, watching my eyes, her fingers following my face like she's attempting to imprint it into her memory. "Em?" I ask unobtrusively.

"Truly dear?"

"I love you," I murmur, watching her eyes flash in the candlelight. She plunges her head and contacts her lips to mine delicately, "I do have one solicitation." I mumble as her lips move my mine and start a moderate strenuous path down my neck to the base of my throat.

"Also, that is?"

"We at any rate examine the chance of you taking my last name, I know the amount of a control crack you are." I feel her giggling against my hot skin before she lifts her head up and raises one of her ideal blonde eyebrows at me.

"I'll consider the big picture, presently pick up the pace and take your garments off before I alter my perspective." Laughing, I cheerfully oblige as we tumble into our own little cut of great.

CPSIA information can be obtained
at www.ICGtesting.com
Printed in the USA
LVHW051641020221
678130LV00003B/340